JUST FOR KICKS

Paul Baczewski

J. B. Lippincott

New York

JUST FOR KICKS
Copyright © 1990 by Paul A. Baczewski

Library of Congress Cataloging-in-Publication Data
Baczewski, Paul.
    Just for kicks / Paul Baczewski.
        p.   cm.
    Summary: Fifteen-year-old Brandon does not suspect
the difficulties in store for him as manager of the varsity
football team when his sister Sarah joins and becomes
the star punter.
    ISBN 0-397-32465-0. — ISBN 0-397-32466-9 (lib. bdg.)
    [1. Football—Fiction.   2. Sex role—Fiction.
3. Brothers and sisters—Fiction.   4. High schools—
Fiction.   5. Schools—Fiction.]   I. Title.
PZ7.B1364Ju   1990   90-30528
[Fic]—dc20   CIP
                                            AC

Typography by David Saylor
10 9 8 7 6 5 4 3 2 1
First Edition

To Sarah,
I hope she plays basketball

JUST FOR
KICKS

CHAPTER 1

Me and my bright ideas.

Looking back on it now, I guess I should have known better. After all, even for age fifteen I'm what you'd have to consider a pretty bright kid. Now, that's not to say that I was entirely at fault. I had lots of help, if you know what I mean. Besides, who could have ever predicted the craziness or the mayhem that was to result from my brilliant suggestion? How was I to know that before we were through, Coach Knox would be acting more like Groucho Marx than Vince Lombardi? Or that we'd wind up squaring off against Vanden High School, the greatest football powerhouse in the state. Or that Sarah and Ferraro . . . Well, maybe I should just start at the beginning.

It all began on a bone-dry Saturday afternoon in late August. John and Jim, my older brothers, were sitting at the kitchen table eating lunch. Actually, they were devouring lunch. Everything is one big competition as far as they're concerned, and from the way they were going after the sandwiches, potato chips and pop, this was no exception.

I quietly closed the refrigerator door. I'd come in hoping to find something to eat, but one quick look inside told me I was too late. It was cleaned out. For a second I actually considered going over to the table and snatching a stray piece of lunch meat or cheese, but the way my brothers were eating you could've lost a couple of fingers just like that, or maybe even an entire hand if you were particularly unlucky. So instead I just hopped up on the counter, grabbed an apple and leaned back to watch feeding time at the zoo.

My brothers were laughing and joking and between hurried gulps talking about football, which was hardly surprising since that's all they ever talk about anyway.

"Yeah," Jim said, stuffing a handful of chips into his mouth, "my favorite time of year. Nothing quite matches that feeling of running around in one-hundred-degree heat while some two-hundred-fifty-pound gorilla tries to rip my head off."

"Poooor baby," cooed John. "Who are you kidding? You love it! All that glory and you try to pretend it's some kind of hardship. I never see you during the season without some gorgeous chick on your arm. And it's a different one every time. Sounds real tough."

Jim sat back in his chair looking smug. "I guess you do have a point. No pain, no gain, huh?"

John shook his head. "I don't think any gain is worth the pain Flymow is going to give us."

Flymow was Mr. Knox, the high school varsity football coach. Coach Knox was an ex-Marine whose hair looked as if it had just graduated from boot camp. Someone had once suggested that the top of his head had been run over by a lawnmower. Someone else said that it must've been a Flymow, since they cut so close to the ground. He'd been Flymow ever since, though never when there was the slightest chance that he might hear it.

"It's really not funny," John continued. "This year Flymow says he's going to turn preseason practice into a survival camp, and anyone who makes it to the regular season in one piece is going to get a little certificate to prove he was one of the 'survivors.' "

"I don't want to be a survivor," Jim moaned. "I just want to be a star football player."

They were right. Coach Knox was brutal. Last

year I was only the water boy, but I had to grow four extra arms and two extra legs just to keep up with the pace he set. Truthfully, I was almost as concerned about the upcoming season as my brothers were. Just about a month earlier I had been summoned to Coach Knox's office down at the school. When I walked in, he looked me square in the eye and set his jaw.

"Son," he said, "I watched you closely last year when you were water boy, and I have to say I liked the pride and dedication you displayed in carrying out your tasks. I also liked the way you hauled that big water jug around. I've given it some thought, and as of this moment you're my team manager. Congratulations."

Standing there, being told this, without any input on my part, I did what any fifteen-year-old, red-blooded American male would have done in that same situation. I fell to my knees, grabbed his hand and kissed his ring. I was grateful. I thought Flymow'd called me into his office to tell me I had to *play* football this year.

"He's going to pick us off, one by one. I just know it," John droned on.

John possesses the eternal pessimism that results from spending one's life as an offensive lineman. There's also something else he possesses as a result— his size. You see, John is huge. I'm talking behemoth.

4

Sitting there at the table, he looked as if he'd just gotten lost on the way to a weight lifters' convention. And it's not the result of a genetic miracle on the part of my parents either. John did it all on his own. Ever since I can remember, his favorite pastime seemed to be the lifting of incredibly heavy objects, which he then threw around the room. Coach Knox calls him dedicated. Jim calls him stupid. I figure he's somewhere in between.

Jim, on the other hand, is everyone's picture of a quarterback. His tall, athletic build and tanned, handsome face set him apart from the rest of us mere mortals. His shaggy blond hair adds to the illusion that he belongs on one of those Southern California beaches where everyone spends his time admiring himself. His personality tells you it's no illusion. It isn't that he's a bad guy; it's just that in his own mind he ranks right up there with the Pope, the President and Bo Jackson.

John is not at all like that. In fact, his humble, quiet demeanor is such a contrast to Jim's that I've always secretly suspected that he was adopted at birth and our parents lied to him so as not to freak him out.

The lunchtime massacre was about over. John was still mumbling to himself about the horrors of the season to come, while Jim demolished the last of the carrot sticks. Suddenly, John shot upright in his chair. "There's only one thing we can do to stop

Flymow," he announced.

"You're right," Jim agreed. "We've got to kill him. How much does it cost to hire a professional assassin? I'll volunteer to help at car washes or sell candy bars to raise the money."

"No, no," John said. "We have only one choice. We're going to have to win the state championship. Anything less and he'll grind us into dust."

Jim began to laugh. "You act as though there's nothing to it. A lot of really great teams never even smell a championship. Remember the team we played on as freshmen? Even they came up short."

I had to agree with Jim. That team won the league and section championships easily and finished second in the state, losing only to the powerful Vanden Vikings in the championship game.

John looked hopeful. "But I'm telling you, I think this year we're as good. We've got it all. We can run. We can throw. Our defense is fabulous. We've got so many good athletes on the team, I don't see how anyone can beat us."

Jim was not convinced. "I don't know. Before we win anything we're going to have to beat Vanden, and that takes a complete, all-around team. Unfortunately, we're lacking one very important thing."

"What?"

"A kicking game."

John slumped down in his chair. "I was hoping you

wouldn't bring that up," he said.

Jim let out a big sigh. "I'm sorry, but our kicking game sucks. Remember last season?"

"Well, maybe Pritchard will do better this year," John said hopefully. "You should see the way he booms those kicks when we're out practicing."

"That's just it," Jim said. "He leaves his best kicks in practice. The minute the pressure's on in a game, he folds up like a tent."

John stared blankly at Jim. A hopeless silence fell over the room. Now, maybe it was none of my business, but the truth is, these guys are so dumb that if their IQs were any lower, they'd have to be watered every day. I mean, I had just heard the front door slam. The answer to all their problems was in the house at that very moment. So, thinking I was doing them a big favor, I finally blurted out, "Why don't you get Sarah to kick for you?"

John just about fell out of his chair laughing. Jim flashed me a look of contempt. "Oh, that's good, real good," he sneered. "Don't you have something better to do, like go out and get hit by a car?"

"I really don't see what the problem is," I said. "You need a kicker, right? Well, where are you going to find one better than Sarah? You remember when she used to go out and play in those pickup games with you guys? She put so many punts into the parking lot that everyone started calling her 'Fender

Bender Sarah.' I'm telling you, she's the one you want."

Jim scoffed. "What do you know about it, shrimp? We're not talking a pickup game here. We're talking playing with the big boys. Besides, she doesn't have the grapes."

"She does too!" I protested, though I felt a little silly arguing about her anatomy. "You just never give her a chance."

"Sarah is pretty good, isn't she?" John mused half to himself.

"Pretty good?" I jumped in. "She used to blow the oleanders out of the ground with her kicks! Remember? After a while the gardener down at the school wouldn't even let her on the field unless she promised to play another position."

I could see that I was getting to John. I could tell because he was holding his head like he'd just pulled a muscle up there. Finally, he scratched his chin and said, "I don't know about you, Jim, but I'm a desperate man."

The pained look on Jim's face revealed that he was as well. He took a deep breath. "Okay, we'll do it."

Well, it just so happened that at that very moment Sarah came bursting into the room. Decked out in a rugby shirt, gray shorts and Nikes, she'd apparently been working out like all the other maniacs around here.

She bounded across the room and over to the refrigerator. Sarah always crosses a room like she's been shot out of a cannon. I don't think it's possible for her to move in any other fashion. On the balls of her feet, with her long, flaming red hair fanned out in waves down her back, she's the perfect picture of a perpetual-motion machine. She's so full of energy that I swear her feet hardly ever touch the ground.

She quickly dove into the refrigerator, looking for something that would help sustain life. As she leaned in among the half-empty jars of mayonnaise, pickles and olives, my brothers stared at her back with an intensity that had them resembling a pair of cats on a fence watching an unwary robin hunt for worms. Sarah must've somehow felt the piercing energy of their collective gaze, because she suddenly froze. "What are you bozos staring at?" she demanded, without even turning around.

When no answer was forthcoming, she spun around to find herself confronting two of the most innocent, angelic faces you've ever seen.

"Hey, Sarah, how's it going?" Jim asked warmly.

Sarah's eyes narrowed with suspicion. "It was going pretty good until now. So, what do you chumps want?"

Jim looked deeply offended. "Is that any way to talk to your loving brothers, who care so deeply for you? We're just happy to see you, that's all."

"Oh, sure, I'll bet," she answered. "I know you guys, so don't try to b.s. me, okay? Just what are you up to?"

"We're not up to anything," Jim said. "We just have a little proposition for you, that's all."

"What sort of proposition?" she asked, eying him warily.

Jim paused for a moment. "Sarah, how about playing football with us?"

Sarah looked slightly puzzled. "That's it? You just want me to play football?"

Jim nodded eagerly.

"Well, I can't," she said. "I'm busy for the rest of the day."

Jim shook his head impatiently. "I'm not talking about today. I'm talking about this year, on the varsity football team."

Sarah's face went stone cold. "Come on, what are you up to?"

"Nothing!" Jim promised. "It's just that we've got a problem with our kicking game and we thought you could help us out."

Sarah gave him a look you might normally reserve for a plate full of raw octopus. "Well, that's ridiculous, so just forget it. I've got better things to do with my time than stand around here and be the butt of your adolescent jokes."

She spun around on her heels and stormed out of the room.

"What a zoo!" she yelled, as she turned the corner and marched down the hall.

"Way to go, Jim," John whined. "What do we do now?"

Jim turned and glared at me. "See, what did I tell you?" He shook his head in disgust. "You and your bright ideas. I don't know why we ever listen to you. Next time you've got something to say, just do us a favor and stick a sock in it, okay?"

Well, I suppose I could have just dropped it right there, but then I'd have to end the story now. No, for some inexplicable reason I didn't drop it. I couldn't. You see, this was the way it had always been. Every time I'd come up with a good idea or I'd try something ambitious, my brothers would land on me like a ton of bricks and wouldn't let up until I'd given up or backed down. Well, maybe I'd just been bullied too long by these clowns, because I vowed that this time would be different. This time I would prove myself, I would carry through to the very end.

I slid down from the counter and leaned toward the opening to the hallway. "Well, you know, guys," I said in a loud voice, "it really was a pretty stupid idea, actually thinking that someone like Sarah could just go right out and make the varsity football team." After that, I simply stood back and let nature take its course.

Sure enough, within seconds, I could hear a rumbling in the distance. I counted down. Five, four, three, two, one. Right on schedule, Sarah exploded into the kitchen and came flying at me. I found myself pressed up against the counter with Sarah's sharp finger embedded in my chest.

"What did you say, punk?" she snarled.

I don't mind telling you, it was a pretty intimidating situation. The top of Sarah's head came up to my nose, which meant her mouth was even with my throat. I was at a very delicate point in my plan. I knew that if I screwed up here, there was a possibility she might lunge forward and rip out my Adam's apple with her bare teeth. What's more, my brothers were watching with rapt interest, which meant they'd surely mop up by slapping me around pretty good for the next week or so.

"Oh, I was just thinking out loud, that's all," I pressed on. "I can understand how you might not want to embarrass yourself in front of all those people. It's probably just as well that you don't come out."

Sarah's eyes widened. "What are you talking about? You know damn well that I'm twice as good a kicker as that choke artist Pritchard. I just don't feel like doing it, that's all."

I was starting to feel a little guilty. This was almost too easy, sort of like stealing candy from a baby. "Yeah, sure, whatever you say, Sarah," I continued, baiting the trap further. "All I know is that it's one thing to go out and play in a pickup game, and it's another to put on the pads and do it under pressure."

Sarah flashed a look of contempt. "Get off it, who are you kidding? There's nothing hard about kicking a football. All it takes is a strong leg."

"Yeah, a strong *male* leg."

"What . . . ? Why, why . . . you — you little —" Sarah's whole body began convulsing while her face turned about ten shades of purple.

Really, I'm not sexist, but it's like they say: You can't make an omelet without first breaking a few eggs. Besides, she stepped into it. All I did was pull the trap door.

It took Sarah a moment to pull herself together again, and when she did, she sputtered, "You little sleazebag, I ought to kick your little *male* butt right now!"

I'd come too far to back down now. I straightened myself up to my full height and said, "Yeah, well, talk is cheap and talk's all I ever hear from you. I've got ten bucks says that when they post that final roster on the locker room door after tryouts, your name will be missing."

Sarah hesitated. I could see she was confused. A hint of desperation flashed across her face. "Why are you doing this?" she hissed.

Good question. I guess because I saw a lot of Sarah in me. I remembered Little League baseball and the

13

way she used to crush the ball until my brothers and their friends ran her out of the league. And on the swim team, she used to destroy everyone, including the guys, until all the dunkings and abuse became too much and she quit. She'd finally been driven to the girls' soccer team—a move that seemed to delight my brothers no end.

Sarah was a great athlete, but she'd always pulled up short, had never taken it to the limits. Maybe I thought that we could both prove something to the two gorillas who were sitting across the room watching like vultures.

Of course, I couldn't tell her this. I simply met her stare with one of my own and said, "Because you've got no guts."

Words cannot adequately describe the look Sarah gave me then. It was somewhere between disbelief and hatred, the sort you might reserve for someone who had just stolen your Springsteen tickets.

"Fine. Have it your way. Only make it twenty dollars, you little worm!" she snarled, as she spun on her heels and swept out of the room in a move so violent that it shook all the walls in the house.

I heaved a big sigh of relief. My entire body tingled. I felt as though I'd just pulled off the crime of the century. My brothers must've felt the same, because they started giggling and laughing and carrying on like a bunch of adolescents, which, of course, they are. Jim picked up the milk carton and poured a round for everyone, including me.

"Here's to the next state championship football team!" he proclaimed.

"Right on!" added John.

I smiled. "It's in the bag!"

"It better be," Jim said, stabbing a finger in my direction. "If anything goes wrong, we'll remember whose idea this was."

The smile vanished from my face.

Me and my bright ideas.

CHAPTER 2

I've often heard it said that when the going gets weird, the weird turn pro. And nowhere was that more evident than in the way my brothers and sister began preparing for the upcoming season.

There were five-mile runs, push-ups, sit-ups, sprints, weight lifting and bleacher running. And after that, long, grueling hours were spent practicing. Sarah practiced her punting. Jim practiced his passing. John practiced being an animal. I practiced eating and resting. You see, my sport didn't begin for months. I'm a basketball player.

That's right, I'm not like all the other animals in

this zoo. Going into my sophomore year, I'm already six-foot-three, and I don't plan to stop growing until I'm worth about ten million dollars. I have a silky-smooth jump shot that I can hit from anywhere, and Mr. Boyd, the basketball coach, said he wants me to try out for the varsity team this year.

I was beginning to have doubts that I'd still be in one piece by then, because as we closed in on the start of football practice, I was taking more and more of a beating at home.

One day, I came out of the kitchen and found myself face to face with John, who was in the hallway, bent over in a lineman's three-point stance. He immediately fired out and buried his shoulder into my ribs, sending me headfirst into the wall. "Nice hit," he mumbled to himself as he stepped over my broken body and into the kitchen.

Whenever Jim saw me, he'd test the strength of his arm by firing a bullet at me with the football he now carried with him at all times. It didn't matter if I was in my room reading, in the bathroom or even in the living room watching TV with Mom and Dad, I had somehow become Jim's personal bull's-eye. Once, Mom even made a really spectacular one-handed, diving grab of a pass that had ricocheted off the side off my head. Thank goodness for Sarah. All she ever did was bare her teeth and snarl as she passed by.

Somewhere along the way, it occurred to me that

Coach Knox was probably not the sort who liked surprises, so I suggested that it might be wise if we spilled our guts about Sarah before the first day of practice. John and Sarah were a little reluctant to put their rear ends on the line so early. Jim, on the other hand, was not about to let on that he was intimidated. He puffed up his chest, and with his best machismo swagger said, "Hey, no sweat. We'll talk to him, he'll agree. He's toast."

Toast. The three of them froze in their tracks. Their eyes met. Suddenly, without warning, as if some hidden common genetic code had been activated, they turned and bolted into the kitchen like wild banshees and began devouring everything in sight. I slumped down in my chair. That's how it is in this family. When the going gets tough, the three of them usually get going.

Fortunately, it didn't take long to come up with a plan. John, Jim and I were to meet Sarah at school on the day before practice began. When Sarah showed up, I hardly recognized her. She wore a pair of beat-up old tennis shoes, faded jeans and a long flannel shirt. Her hair was tucked up under a New York Yankee's baseball cap. It was a great disguise. She looked just like any one of the guys who'd come down to get in a last-minute workout on the weights or to run a few laps around the track.

We were hoping to sneak Sarah through the boys'

locker room and up into Coach Knox's office unnoticed. Sarah didn't seem too excited about the whole thing. "Are you sure this is going to work?" she asked uneasily.

"What's the matter, Sis, you chickening out? Going to throw in the towel so soon?" Jim said.

I stepped forward. "Chill out, Jim. Nobody's going to chicken out." I turned to Sarah. "We just need a few minutes to talk to Flymow before we tell him who you really are," I reassured her. "Now, John's going to go in and make sure the locker room's empty, then we'll make our move, okay?"

Sarah still looked a little skeptical, but she finally agreed. "Well, all right."

On cue, John disappeared inside the locker room. After a few minutes he reappeared. "The coast is clear," he reported.

Jim turned to me. "So what are you waiting for, shorty?" he said, as he pushed me forward through the double doors. "This was your idea, remember?"

I had never been the lead guide for a suicide mission before, so I wasn't exactly sure what my job was at this point. But two things did pop into my head. The first was that the shortest distance between two points is a straight line. The second was a quote I'd heard somewhere. "If it were done when 'tis done, then 'twere well it were done quickly." With those two thoughts in mind, I cut a beeline through the

19

long, narrow corridor of lockers, my eyes firmly fixed on the door of Coach Knox's office up ahead.

Suddenly, seemingly out of thin air, Leroy Davis materialized in front of me. He's like that. He's a running back on the football team and defensive players are forever trying to hit Leroy in the spot he has just vacated, which means he tends to gain a lot of yards. The only problem with his magic act right now was that he'd just gotten out of the shower, and so wasn't wearing anything but the white towel that hung around his neck.

"Say, man, what's goin' on?" he asked.

I froze in my tracks, which brought our whole procession to an immediate halt. Right behind me, Sarah let out a huge gasp.

John pushed past me, grabbed Leroy by the shoulders and tossed him back through the narrow opening between the lockers that led to the shower.

"Hey, watch it!" Leroy protested indignantly as he went tumbling backward.

"Sorry, man," John apologized. "But just do me a favor and stay there for a second, okay?"

John looked a touch out of control, so Leroy wasn't too anxious to press him further on the subject. "Anything you say, big man."

John stepped back, grabbed Sarah by the elbow and hauled her past while she struggled to turn her head backward and get one last peek. "C'mon, let's go!" he ordered.

We hustled the rest of the way down the corridor and up the stairs to the office. There we hesitated until Jim finally stepped forward and knocked on the door.

"Come in!" a voice boomed from within.

We all meekly filed in to find Coach Knox standing across the room, bare-chested, wearing a pair of faded green sweatpants that were drenched with perspiration. He had obviously just finished a major workout of his own.

Coach Knox is a very impressive physical specimen. He stands about five foot ten, and every muscle in his body is well defined. Not only does it look like he was chiseled out of granite, it looks as if he wore out four or five sculptors in the process. He's such a fanatic about conditioning that it makes me thankful he isn't my coach. In fact, the biggest compliment he can give someone is to slap him hard on the back and proudly proclaim, "Son, you'd make one heck of a Marine!" It's no wonder the guys on the football team weren't too thrilled about him.

Coach Knox nodded at us as he opened his locker and pulled out an immaculately clean white towel and a bottle of shampoo. As we stood there, engulfed in an uneasy silence, I got the queasy feeling that he was about to do something that we'd all be sorry for. I was right.

At that very moment, Coach Knox reached down to remove his sweatpants. Sarah looked like she was about to faint. I felt like I was about to die.

"You guys just wait here for a second while I grab a quick shower," he said.

Jim spoke right up, urgency in his voice. "Wait a minute, Coach! Don't do that! We've got to talk to you about something."

Coach Knox looked down at his hands, which were at his waist, then back at Jim. "We'll talk in a minute, son. First, let me get out of these sweaty things."

"But you can't do that, Coach!"

He looked genuinely perplexed. "Can't do what, son?"

"You can't take your sweats off!" Jim sputtered.

Coach Knox just stared at him blankly.

Jim groaned. "No . . . no, that's not what I mean. Of course you can take your sweats off, but not right now. No, I . . . I mean, you could take them off right now if you wanted to, but I don't think you really want to." By this time, Jim had pretty much managed to confuse everyone, including himself. He took a deep breath. "I guess what I'm trying to say is that we've got to talk to you about something really important."

A look of concern crept across Coach Knox's face. I could see he was trying to figure out just how his star quarterback had managed to lose all his brains over one short summer. "Well, spit it out, son, what's the problem?"

Jim brightened. "It's really not a problem, sir. It's just that we've found a kicker for the football team."

Somehow this earth-shattering news failed to have its intended effect on Coach Knox. "That's it?" he asked. "That's what this whole thing's all about? You've found a kicker?"

"Yes, sir!" Jim said as he dragged Sarah forward. "We've come up with the best darn kicker in the entire county!"

Coach Knox looked her over for a moment. "That's nice. Very nice," he finally said. "Have him come around tomorrow and try out like everyone else, okay?" He began to pull down his sweatpants. "Is it all right if I get back to my shower now?"

"Wait!" Jim cried. "Please don't do that, sir!"

"What is it now?" Coach yelled as he straightened up.

"Well, it's just that we have something else to tell you."

"I was afraid of that." Coach Knox rolled his eyes toward the ceiling. "Why is it that I have the feeling I'm never going to get clean?"

Jim grimaced. "I don't quite know how to put this, sir, but he's not a he."

Coach Knox stared down at the floor. "He's not a

he," he repeated slowly. He then shook his head, undoubtedly concerned that he was going to be forced to administer a urine test to find out which drugs Jim had been using. "What are you jabbering about, son? Who's not a he?"

Jim swallowed hard. "He's not," he said, pointing to Sarah.

"He's not?" Coach Knox asked. "Well, tell me, son, if he's not a he, then just what in the heck is he?"

I guess you could say we had reached crunch time. That's the point in the game where you either make the play that wins it or you screw up and go home in defeat. Jim did what any quarterback would have done in the same situation; he looked over in our direction, frantically searching for someone to hand off to.

Since none of us were running backs, we did our best to avoid his desperate gaze. Sarah hunched down into her shirt as far as she could go. All you could see of her head were two little pink ears that stuck out between her collar and baseball cap. I pretended to be reading about the exploits of a football team from years past, which were immortalized in some old, faded newspaper clippings that hung from a bulletin board on the wall. John stared down at his feet, pawing the linoleum like a horse who has learned to count.

Jim had no choice but to continue on alone.

"Well, you see, sir," he began. "What he is, sir, is . . . well . . ."

"Well?" Coach Knox demanded.

"Uh . . . Uh . . . Uh . . . Uh . . ."

Terminal gridlock. Wouldn't you know it. And with Coach Knox rapidly losing patience it was quite apparent we were all going to die. So I did the only thing I could.

I lunged forward. "He's our sister!" I blurted as I pulled the cap off Sarah's head and sent her hair billowing down like a slow-motion avalanche.

That revelation went over about as well as you might have expected. Coach Knox's eyes got real big, and he hippy-hopped backward. With one quick sweep of the arm he grabbed his gray sweatshirt off the floor and scrambled into it in what must've been world-record time.

"Just what is going on here?" he bellowed.

Jim's mouth began to function again. "I . . . it . . . it's like I was trying to tell you, Coach, we figured the team needed a kicker, so . . ."

Coach Knox cut him off. "You thought you'd come up here and make a fool of me, didn't you?"

"No, sir, that's not it at all."

"I want to know who put you up to this."

"No one! If you'd just listen for a minute, I'd . . ."

Coach Knox hit himself in the forehead with the

palm of his hand. "Of course! It must've been Boyd! Ever since that time I sprayed stickum all over the basketballs, he's been out to get me. You should have seen those kids trying to shoot free throws! I laughed so hard I darn near busted a gut." He chuckled to himself. "Well, he really got me good this time, that old son of a . . ."

"No, sir," Jim interrupted. "He had nothing to do with it. It was all our idea. Actually, it was Brandon's idea, but that's beside the point. We need a kicker, and Sarah's about ten times better than Pritchard or anyone else we're going to find."

Coach Knox stared at Jim in amazement. "You're serious about this, aren't you?"

"That's what I've been trying to tell you!" Jim exclaimed.

"Well, I just don't understand what you're getting so worked up about, son," he said. "Our problem in those losses last year wasn't Pritchard. It was poor conditioning and a lack of intensity. That's some- thing we're going to work on this year. We should never have to depend on a kicker to save our bacon."

"This is ridiculous!" Sarah finally said. "C'mon, let's blow this pop stand."

Coach Knox looked pleased. "That's right, listen to your sister. Football is about smashing mouths, not kicking. It's a man's game, it's not for little girls."

Whether he knew it or not, Coach Knox had just

made a mistake of enormous proportions. I never really knew what the term "hopping mad" meant until that moment. Sarah's body could hardly contain her anger as she seemed to levitate off the ground, her feet shuffling all the while.

"A man's game!" she yelled. "A man's game? Do you hear this chump? Look here, fella. First of all, I can kick the butt of just about any one of those big, burly males you've got on your team. Me and my brothers have been doing it for years. And second, anyone with half a brain knows how important kicking is. Why, if you keep someone pinned deep in their own territory long enough, they're bound to make a mistake. When they do, bam, you convert it into a quick score." She shook her head in disgust. "You know, if I knew as little about football as you obviously do, I'd be ashamed to admit it. It's no wonder you've never won a state championship."

No one moved. We were all frozen in a state of shock, none more so than Coach Knox, whose mouth hung open so wide you could've stuffed an entire Big Mac in it and still had room left over for fries.

"Just a minute here, young lady," he finally said, in a voice so stern that the room temperature dropped a good ten degrees. "No one's spoken to me like that since back in boot camp." He cocked his head and narrowed his eyes. "So you think you're pretty good, do you?"

Sarah met his cold hard stare with one of her own. "As good as you're going to find around here."

Coach Knox began stroking his chin with his fingers. "Well, if you want to come out for the team that badly, then go ahead, I don't care." The smallest trace of a smile crept onto his face. "But I warn you, I intend to bust your butt, Miss Women's Lib. You understand?"

Sarah's eyes were still locked with his. "I wouldn't have it any other way, Flymow."

Flymow! Oh boy, you could see Coach Knox trying hard to figure that one out. John began whistling and looked up at the ceiling, while Jim bent down to tie a shoelace that was already firmly knotted.

"Well," Coach Knox finally said, "I expect to see you all here tomorrow morning at seven sharp for equipment issue." He narrowed his eyes at me. "He's our sister," he mimicked. "That's good, son, real good. *You* be here at six to help me get things organized. We'll see how funny you are at the crack of dawn." He pressed his eyes shut and began rubbing his forehead with one hand. "Now, all of you, get out of here and leave me alone."

Well, I guess you could say it was our turn to stand around gaping like idiots. He'd actually agreed to it!

Coach Knox opened his eyes to find us still there. "I said get out of here!" he yelled. "And I meant it! Now get!"

28

As the old saying goes, we didn't let the door hit us on the backside as we sprinted out of his office, down the stairs and through the locker room. By the time we got outside, we were gasping for air from a combination of terror, excitement and just plain hard running. My brothers began a wild victory dance as Sarah looked on, disgusted. I heaved a big sigh of relief. We'd hurdled, however narrowly, the first barrier. I could already see that this was going to be a lot more difficult than it had looked. For better or worse, the fun was just beginning.

CHAPTER 3

The next morning, I arose at the crack of dawn and staggered blearily down to the school. When I arrived there, I was surprised to find the double doors of the locker room already propped open and the lights inside turned on. I stepped in and looked around. The place seemed to be deserted. The only sounds I could hear as I moved through the room were the erratic dripping of water from the shower heads and the squeaking of my sneakers as they shuffled along the cold concrete floor.

When I reached the equipment room, I was greeted by a shocking sight. The top half of its Dutch door was open, and I could see that everything had already been laid out inside. Rows of shiny helmets hung from the walls. Practice pants and jerseys were neatly folded on a large, brown table in the center of the room. Shoulder pads sat on the floor, arranged in a precise circle around the room. Inside the door stood a card table, upon which rested an open ledger with the names of all the players already written out and columns marked off for checking out the equipment.

I couldn't believe it. Everything was so well organized, it made me wonder what kind of idiot would've been crazy enough to get there earlier than me just to do all that.

Just then, I heard the slapping of feet on pavement and heavy breathing ring through the hallway. I turned around as Coach Knox ran up, his face slightly red and his shirt and shorts darkened with sweat. My question had been answered.

"Good morning, son," he said as he came to a stop, grabbed his left wrist and began checking his pulse. He took a series of long, deep breaths, then said, "I'll tell you, there's nothing quite like a good, hard five-mile run first thing in the morning to get that old blood pumping. Say, you're an athlete, aren't you? Why don't you come out tomorrow and join me?"

I'd had my doubts about Coach Knox before, but now I knew for sure: He was mad as a hatter. "Uh, gee, no thanks, Coach. I'd really like to, but,

31

um . . . I've got this condition."

"What condition?"

"Uh, yeah, it's this thing where every time I run about five miles, my legs get tired, my lungs start to ache and I run out of breath. It's a real unpleasant feeling."

Coach Knox looked concerned. "That sounds unnatural, son. You should have it checked out by a doctor."

"I will, sir," I agreed, remembering that it's always best to humor a madman.

With that, I set to work. Appearances notwithstanding, there were still a surprising number of tasks to accomplish, and as is so often the case, it seemed like I'd barely begun when the players began drifting in. The otherworldly silence of the previous hour was rapidly replaced by a raucous din as the room filled.

I'd barely finished stocking the first-aid chest when Coach Knox called me over. "Okay, everybody," he announced to the gathering, "I want this to go as quickly and orderly as possible, so let's stop the horseplay and listen up." The room instantly fell silent. He put his hands on his hips and presented his best field-general look. "Now, you are each about to be issued a helmet, shoulder pads, jersey, pants, girdle and socks. I expect every one of you to take proper care of this equipment. That means not sitting on your helmets on the sidelines or modifying your shoulder pads to make them lighter. And yes, Crozier, that also means washing it all more than once this season."

The guys all around Roger Crozier broke out in laughter and gave him gentle nudges in the back and elbows in the ribs. Crozier responded with a small, embarrassed smile. You see, walking within ten feet of him was a hazardous undertaking at best. He was a defensive lineman who smelled so bad that Coach Knox had been forced to create a rule where he was not allowed to raise his arms when rushing the passer in practice. The problem was, every time he did, the entire offensive line and the quarterback passed out from the noxious odor. It was kind of an unfair advantage, so he'd been told to save it for the real game.

Coach Knox clapped his hands together. "Okay, let's begin." He motioned down the hallway. "I want everybody in one line against this wall."

But before anyone had a chance to move, a slight commotion began at the back of the room. It slowly moved forward through the sea of players, and by the time Jim, John and Sarah popped out of the crowd the whole place was buzzing. Players all around stared at Sarah in bewilderment. As Jim surveyed the scene, a large, devilish smile grew on his face. He looked downright proud of himself. "Hi, Coach," he said cheerfully. "We thought it would be a good idea if Sarah got her equipment first. That way she could get out of here before anyone started to undress. You know what I mean?"

It sounded as though a million jabbering monkeys had instantly materialized in the room as the buzz turned into a full-scale uproar. Players began laughing, crying, stammering and in general making assorted other guttural sounds. Coach Knox, however, remained cool as a cucumber. "I told you all to get in line!" he barked. "Now shut up and do it!"

The only sound that could be heard from that point on was the frantic scrambling of feet as the players dove for their places against the wall. Having accomplished that, Coach Knox turned to Sarah. "Well, well, look what we have here. Little Miss Foots was serious about playing with the big boys after all."

A few of the players in the background giggled. Sarah straightened up and stuck out her jaw. "C'mon, Flymow, just give me some equipment so we can get this show on the road, okay?"

As Sarah followed Coach Knox into the equipment room, the team leaped to fall in behind her, pushing and shoving one another as they crowded around the doorway in an attempt to get a better view.

Coach Knox moved swiftly. Within minutes, he'd loaded Sarah down with gear. As she walked to the door, he handed her a pen and pointed to the ledger. She carefully balanced her load in one arm and hurriedly scribbled her signature across the page. When she handed Coach Knox back his pen, their eyes met once again.

"I'm going to make your life miserable, Foots," he promised.

Sarah glanced over at the players milling around the doorway. Then she looked at me thoughtfully. I swallowed hard. Our first big test. Then she winked, turned to Coach Knox and smiled. "Well, you just give it your best shot, big guy."

Sarah turned to leave. The team backed away from the door and parted like the Red Sea. Each head swiveled as Sarah bounded by until everyone in the place was facing backward, witnessing, in stunned silence, her exit from the locker room.

"What are you all staring at?" Coach Knox yelled once she was gone. "We haven't got all day, so let's get a move on!"

Everyone got his gear quickly, and before I knew it, I was headed out to the practice field, dragging the first-aid kit and a sack of footballs behind me. I was accompanied by Timmy Nelson, who swayed awkwardly as he struggled with a large and rather heavy water jug. He was doing the "rookie run." Since there was too much equipment for me to carry out all at once, every day someone who was new to the team, a "rookie," was assigned the task of helping me. It was supposed to be the ultimate humiliation, and maybe for some it was, but right now Timmy looked a lot more scared than embarrassed.

"Do you think it's going to be as bad out there as everyone says?" he asked, his voice trembling.

I figured I should level with the poor guy. "I think it's going to be a lot worse than that."

His eyes got real big and his mouth began moving rapidly, although no words emerged. He tripped over the water jug and crashed to the ground. "Worse?" he squeaked, while lying flat on his back. "What do you mean?"

I reached down, grabbed his arm and helped him up. "Coach Knox is obsessed with the thought of winning the state championship," I explained. "He's never done it, and now he has this crazy notion that if he works this team harder than any he's had in the past, it might make a difference."

Timmy gulped and shrank about two inches. I felt sorry for him. He was only about five foot five and a hundred twenty pounds, the perfect size for winding up as nothing more than a tackling dummy. "Say, Timmy," I asked out of curiosity, "what made you decide to come out for the team, anyway?"

Timmy meekly shrugged. "My dad, I guess. He's been after me for years to play football. He says it'll help make a man out of me, though I don't know how that's going to happen if it kills me when I'm still a boy."

"Don't worry, I think you'll do just fine," I said,

although I really didn't believe it. "Just remember that Coach Knox usually lets up once everyone starts puking."

"What!" he screamed. "Puking? What are you talking about? No one said anything about puking!"

Practice hadn't even begun and already Timmy was losing it. This did not bode well for his future. And to make matters worse, we arrived at the practice field just in time to see Ron Ferraro claim his first victim.

Ferraro was the team's all-everything linebacker who just loved to hit: people, dogs, trees, it didn't matter. If it was standing, you could bet that he'd make sure it wound up flat on the ground.

Unfortunately for those around him, his favorite pastime was to come up to someone who wasn't paying attention, grab his face mask, then slam his forehead into theirs. This generally caused the person who'd been blasted to find himself instantly up to his nose in grass, wallowing around on all fours with all the mental and physical capacity of an earthworm.

Ferraro had just unloaded this "sleeper" hit on some poor, scrawny, little guy who now lay on the ground in a fetal position, his scrambled brains undoubtedly wanting to know why his parents had bothered to bring him into the world if this was the way he was destined to go out.

Timmy dropped to his knees and began to moan.

Sympathy pains; another bad sign. The guys standing around Ferraro all roared with laughter while slapping him roughly on the back, probably praying all the while that none of them would be next. Just then, a loud whistle pierced the air. Coach Knox had arrived on the scene. "Okay, everybody, fall in over here!"

I walked over to the poor guy who still lay prone on the ground and pulled him to his feet. "C'mon," I said, motioning to the large semicircle that was forming around Coach Knox.

"No, no, I've had enough," the guy said, backing away. "I think my mom was right. I would be better off playing tuba in the pep band." He turned and sprinted back toward the locker room.

"There's something I want to say before we get started," Coach Knox announced, stuffing the whistle into the pocket of his black shorts. He set a stern look on his face. "Pride and dedication, gentlemen, remember those two words. They are the foundation upon which everything is built. It's a war out here, and it takes great courage to survive. I think you'll find that it's pride and dedication that will fuel our hearts and strengthen our resolve as we strive to attain success on this noble battlefield. But nothing comes easy. Not here, or anywhere else in life. Success requires, even demands, hard work." Coach Knox's cadence was picking up, the intensity increasing with each sentence. All eyes were glued to him with the exception of Ferraro, who occasionally flashed sidelong glances over at Sarah.

"This year, gentlemen," he continued, "we are going back to basics. This year we are going to play good, old-fashioned football. That means we are going to physically dominate other teams. And we are going to accomplish this through hard work. We are going to accomplish this by becoming the most intense and finely conditioned team this state has ever seen. Do I make myself clear?"

"Yes, sir," a few scattered voices called out.

"What was that?" Coach Knox demanded.

"Yes, sir!" the entire team yelled in unison.

"I can't hear you!" he roared back.

"Yes, sir!" they screamed even louder.

"Who's going to be the hardest-hitting . . ."

"We are!"

". . . the best-conditioned . . ."

"We are!!"

". . . the most dedicated team this state has ever seen!?"

"We are!!!"

The players broke into cheering and clapping as Coach Knox walked in among them, slapping them on the shoulders and on the helmets, secure in the knowledge that he'd sufficiently motivated these young boys into doing incredibly stupid things to their bodies. "Are there any questions?" he asked.

Ron Ferraro quickly spoke up. "Yeah, Coach, I've got one." He pointed over at Sarah. "It's bad enough that we've got to play on the same field with so many wimpy little guys. You going to make us start playing with girls, too?"

Coach Knox looked at Sarah and smiled. "I guess that's the price we have to pay for living in a so-called liberated society, Ferraro. But don't worry, I have a feeling that old Foots here has bitten off a little more than she can chew."

Sarah snarled. "Keep flapping your lips, Flymow, and I'll show you how much I can chew right now."

Coach Knox nodded his head. "Oh, that's good, Foots, very good. I like that. A little spirit, a little fire. What do you say, Ferraro? Wouldn't you like the opportunity to show Foots what real football's all about?"

Ferraro's eyes lit up at the thought of a potential new victim. "Yeah, I see what you mean, Coach." He gave Sarah a toothy grin. "Glad to have you aboard."

"Up yours," Sarah shot back.

Coach Knox just smiled. "Ah, that's music to my ears. I just love the start of football season." He looked around. "I'm glad we got that settled. Are there any other questions?"

None were forthcoming. Without warning, his expression changed. "So?! What are you waiting for? Let's move it! Now! Line up for calisthenics!"

The players slowly spread out along the yard lines, about four rows deep and an arm's length apart. "Jim Lewis and Ron Ferraro, front and center! Run this team through the warm-up," Coach Knox ordered.

The two of them could hardly contain themselves. Being called on to lead the exercises meant that Coach Knox had chosen them to be the team captains. This was quite an honor, kind of like being chosen the first ones up the hill during a raid on a machine-gun nest.

As Ron and Jim put the team through their paces, Coach Knox walked up and down the rows, hands clasped behind his back, carefully eying every movement and not saying a word, like a drill sergeant inspecting the new recruits. When the exercises had been completed, Coach Knox walked over to Sarah.

"Well, Foots, did we have a good summer?" he said, smiling sweetly. "Did we remember to get in shape? After all, this isn't girls' soccer."

"Don't worry about me, Flymow, I can take care of myself."

"Good, good, that's what I was hoping to hear." He turned to me and yelled, "Brandon, get the bags!"

I was stunned. I was horrified. I couldn't believe my ears. He wouldn't, not the very first thing on the very first day of practice. "You . . . you mean . . ."

"Yes, son. Get the bags out of the shed. We're going to run the Burma Road."

CHAPTER 4

The Burma Road, oh boy. This drill was unquestion-
ably invented by someone who was trying to improve
on capital punishment. It was obvious Coach Knox
was trying to make a point, and from the way everyone on the team glared, they thought the point was
Sarah.

Not that I could blame them either, because what
happens in the Burma Road is not a pretty sight. In
this drill half the players line up on alternating hash
marks, every five yards for the length of the field,
each holding a blocking bag. Everyone else lines up
along the goal line. On the whistle, the first guy in line

sprints toward the first bag and throws his body into it as hard as he can. After wiping out the first target, he scrambles to his feet and sprints back across the field, at an angle, and launches himself into the next bag. Having scored a direct hit there, he moves on, at which point the whistle blows again and the second person begins, followed moments later by the third, and so on until everyone is involved and the line of players resembles a long, winding serpent, unleashing mayhem on its destructive journey down the field. Once all these players have run the gauntlet, things switch around, allowing the other half of the team to get their revenge for having been unmercifully pounded into the turf while standing there defenseless.

As I began pulling bags out of the shed, I felt a pang of guilt. It was kind of like being asked to load the guns that are going to be used in an execution. But then I remembered that I had already invested a fair amount of my reputation in having Sarah come out. And for the first time it dawned on me that there'd be serious personal consequences to face if this team fell short.

First, I'd have to deal with my brothers. That would be tough, but I've never heard of anyone dying from black eyes, so I'd probably survive that. Then there'd be Coach Knox. A couple of twenty-mile forced marches through the woods in the dead of winter would probably satisfy him. After that, I'd have Sarah to face . . . hmmm, I could see where I had an obligation to help get this team in as good a physical condition as possible. The guilt vanished immediately, and I pulled out the heavyweight bags instead of the light ones.

Within minutes, I had all twenty bags out on the field and ready for action. Some of the players hung back while others slowly meandered over and picked one up. Soon all the bags were accounted for and the players began moving to their places along the hash marks. Timmy Nelson wrestled with a bag that was about the same size as he was, finally dragging it over to the closest open spot available. My mouth dropped open when I realized he was setting up at the first location, right on the five-yard line.

Coach Knox walked over to the group on the goal line. "I want to see some hurt put on those bags! Do I make myself clear?" He raised the whistle to his lips and blew. "Go!"

Poor Timmy never had a chance. John was first in line, and he charged forward like a bull who'd just seen a red flag. When he hit the bag, there was a loud, sharp crack that echoed across the field. The bag went one way, Timmy the other, and his two shoes shot straight up into the air. He flew backward about ten feet before landing in a heap. While he lay on the ground, trying to figure out which planet he was on,

Coach Knox started yelling. "Get your butt off the ground, son! You're holding up the whole drill!"

Timmy slowly climbed to his feet and grabbed his shoes, forcing the right one on his left foot and the left one on the right. He staggered over, picked up the bag and dragged it and himself back into position. The instant he got there, the whistle blew. "Go!" Coach Knox yelled.

Unfortunately for Timmy, Ferraro was next in line. Timmy was a little better prepared this time. His shoulder was up against the bag, his teeth were clenched tightly together and his eyes were pressed shut. But it didn't help—he was once again sent airborne as Ferraro plowed viciously into the bag. This time, when Timmy finally made it to his feet, his helmet was turned sideways and he was looking out the ear hole. I could tell he was dazed and confused because he did nothing to correct the problem. He just picked up his bag again and wandered around in gradually wider circles until he finally managed to stumble across his position again. He probably figured he'd just had an eye knocked out and didn't have the nerve to say anything about it.

Needless to say, this little exhibition did not please Coach Knox. "No, no, son, you're screwing up everything!" He marched over, grabbed Timmy by the head and yanked his helmet around so that it sat correctly on his head.

"C'mere, son," he said as he grabbed Timmy under the arm and pulled him forward. "Let me show you something." He picked up the bag, crouched down behind it and hollered, "C'mon, let's go! I want to see you hit this bag with some authority!"

The next person in line was Bob Pritchard, the team's punter. He happened to be a powder puff when it came to hitting, but since it was the first day of practice he simply gave a slight shrug of the shoulders, as if to say, what the heck, and started his sprint. He was just a matter of inches from making contact when Coach Knox suddenly threw his entire body forward and slammed the bag, with explosive force, into his face. All the momentum that had been moving forward instantaneously moved straight down and Pritchard slammed into the ground.

"You see, son, that's how you do it. Now, get your shoulder into it this time." Coach Knox tossed the bag back at Timmy, who just stared at him in amazement.

The drill started up again, and within minutes the entire field was in motion, alive with grunts, groans and blood-curdling screams. I looked downfield just in time to see Sarah, who was crouched behind a bag, preparing to take a hit from Ferraro. Sarah braced herself, but she was no match for that animal. She went tumbling head over heels as he laid a perfect hit on the middle of the bag.

She got her opportunity for revenge, though, moments later when Coach Knox had everyone switch places. When Sarah came across Ferraro, instead of going for the bag, she went for him, catching him totally off-guard as she buried her helmet into his Adam's apple. Ferraro crashed heavily to the ground and let out a sound that you might expect to hear coming from someone who's had his eyes poked out by a flaming, red-hot iron rod.

This caught Coach Knox's attention. He turned around and saw Ferraro writhing in agony. "All right, all right!" he exclaimed. "We've finally got some decent hitting going on around here!"

On Ron's next trip through you could tell from the intense look in his eyes that he intended to punish Sarah. He destroyed everything in sight, and by the time he got to her he was moving like a runaway locomotive. He exploded toward the bag, at which point Sarah calmly stepped sideways, taking the bag with her. Ferraro's arms and legs pinwheeled frantically as he shot by her, and it seemed as though the entire earth shook when he finally crash-landed, sending chalk, grass and dirt off in all directions as he awkwardly skidded along on his face. Rising to his feet, he furiously grabbed at the huge chunks of turf that had wedged into his face mask. He turned and blasted Sarah with a malevolent glare. Sarah responded by sticking out her tongue. It made me feel good. I could see they were starting to like one another.

Then it happened. Coach Knox's piercing whistle blew an end to the drill. "Pritchard! Foots!" he yelled. "Get over here! I want to see some punting!"

This was the big moment. There was a buzz of anticipation as they headed out to the middle of the field. Jim and John were all smiles. They were keenly aware of Sarah's talent and had taken the opportunity to get down some heavy bets.

Coach Knox quickly assembled the team into punt and punt-return units. He sent Leroy Davis downfield to serve as the punt returner. Turning to Sarah and Pritchard, he said, "Okay, this is live. The two of you will alternate kicks. We'll start with you, Pritchard. Get in there."

Pritchard looked a little nervous as he lined up in his position, fifteen yards behind the center. When the ball arrived, he took two long strides forward, then dropped the ball softly, catching it on the top of his foot. The ball rose in a nice, high trajectory and traveled quite a distance, with Leroy pulling it in about forty-five yards downfield.

"All right!" "Way to go!" Cries erupted from the sideline as the guys cheered him on. Jim and John were not among them. They looked over at me as if demanding an answer, but what could I say? It was just like him to kick great in practice when he always chumped out in games. Pritchard looked relieved, and a big grin appeared on his face.

Sarah stepped in. She rubbed her hands down the side of her pants, then thrust them forward, as if to command the ball to appear. It came and she stepped forward, but, unfortunately, she connected with the back half of the ball and sent it cartwheeling end over end, a "wounded duck" as they say. Leroy had to sprint upfield to make a shoestring catch. The kick was only good for about thirty yards.

Cries of derision echoed across the field. Players sprinted over to Jim and John, slapped them roughly on their backs and tried to double their bets.

Pritchard looked totally relaxed as he stepped in again. His confidence had picked up, and his kick reflected it. He unleashed what was probably the punt of his life, a towering, driving boot that sent Leroy backpedaling until he hauled it in sixty yards downfield. Pritchard made a fist and pumped it up and down in a gesture of triumph.

Along the sideline the guys went crazy, giving each other high fives and pointing at Jim and John. Jim buried his face in his hands. John stared across the field at me, displaying with sign language all the things he intended to do once he got his hands on me. I had now progressed past the point of concerned, by-passed scared entirely and was rapidly closing in on panic.

Sarah looked over in my direction. Determination was etched on her face. With the slightest nod of her head she seemed to indicate that she had things firmly under control, that it was time to send a message. Goose bumps grew on my arm. I knew we were onto something special.

Of course, I was taking no chances. As soon as Sarah stepped into position, I fell to my knees, crossed myself and promised the heavens that I would never again steal my father's *Sports Illustrated* swimsuit issue if they'd just bail me out this one time.

Well, whoever said that God was dead had it all wrong, because this time Sarah's punt soared through the sky, sailing higher and higher, forcing Leroy to scamper back until he made an over-the-shoulder catch some sixty-five yards away.

The entire place fell so quiet that I could hear Pritchard as he let out a large gulp. His face turned pale, and his hands trembled as he took the next snap from center. I'm surprised he was able to make contact at all, though that's about all he did. He popped the ball straight up in the air, directly above his head. He stood frozen in place and stared as the ball turned over and came down with the point hitting him right smack in the face. The team groaned, Sarah laughed, Jim and John exchanged knowing looks and Coach Knox shook his head in disgust.

As Pritchard crawled off to one side, Sarah unleashed a punt unlike anything anyone had ever seen before. The team let out a collective moan as they followed its passage across the sky. Coach Knox's jaw dropped, the whistle fell from his mouth and his clipboard hit the ground. Leroy didn't move an inch. He simply stood and watched the ball, bending farther and farther backward as it passed overhead, until at last he fell over.

The ball completely left the field of play, split the uprights of the goal post and continued on until it tore into the oleanders that grew along the chain-link fence that bordered the school grounds. It blasted one of the flowery bushes out of the ground, roots and all, and settled into the crater that had been created. Sarah turned and smiled serenely at Coach Knox. "What do you think, Flymow? Have I got the job?"

Coach Knox's eyes began darting up and down. He reached down, began fumbling with his whistle and with great effort managed to get it to his lips. "I want to see some pressure put on the punter this time!" he yelled through the piercing shriek. "If I don't see a blocked punt real soon, you'll all find yourselves on that goal line running till I get tired of watching. Do I make myself clear?"

That certainly got everyone's attention. A collective look of desperation settled on the faces of the defensive players as they lined up for the next punt. Luckily for them, due to the rotation of players in and out, Ferraro found himself lined up opposite Timmy Nelson.

Sarah never had a chance. The instant the ball was snapped, Ferraro ran over Timmy and launched himself at her. As Sarah made contact with the ball, Ferraro made contact with Sarah. The ball bounced crazily off his shoulder pad, and the two of them crashed heavily to the ground.

They lay motionless for a moment, their arms and legs intertwined. Finally, Ferraro maneuvered his body around, lifted his head and peered into Sarah's face mask. "Hey, baby," he drawled. "How would you like to go out with me Friday night?"

Sarah responded rather emphatically by thrusting two of her fingers through Ferraro's face mask and into his eyes. He instantly levitated off her and onto the ground, where he rolled around in agony. Sarah got up, dusted herself off and glanced down at Ferraro with disdain before stalking away in Nelson's direction.

She reached Timmy at about the same time he made it back to his feet. She immediately tore into him. "Just what do you think you're doing?" she yelled. "You're supposed to block him, not put an airmail stamp on him!"

Timmy cringed. "Well, he's a lot bigger than me. What do you want me to do?"

Sarah blew up. "I want you to do your job!! That's

what we're all out here for!"

Timmy shrank down until he almost disappeared. He looked like he was about to cry. Sarah watched with a mixture of pity and irritation. "Look," she said at last, her tone softer. "If you don't stand up to guys like these, they'll run you right off the field. I speak from experience. Now I know there's no way you can go head-on with that big goon over there, so you've got to use your brains instead." Sarah took a couple of steps backward. "C'mon, take a run at me."

Timmy looked more than a little suspicious, but Sarah motioned him to come toward her, so he finally put his head down and charged. An instant before impact, Sarah dropped down and rolled into his legs, sending him flying to the turf.

She jumped back up. "You see, a cut block. It's the great equalizer. You don't need to be anywhere as big as the other guy to bring him down with that, and I should know, right?" She reached down, grabbed Timmy by the pads and hoisted him to his feet. "The point is, you can always make the other guy's speed and momentum work to your advantage."

It took a moment, but soon what Sarah had been saying seemed to sink in. A smile grew until it completely covered Timmy's face. Sarah walked over and slapped him on the back, almost knocking him down again, then the two of them ran over to rejoin the group in the middle of the field.

Coach Knox watched all this with the look of someone about to throw up. With one hand he began massaging his temple. He raised his whistle and blew an end to practice before she had the chance to lay waste to his entire team.

As I gathered up the equipment, I was feeling pretty good. It looked like the great experiment was going to work. I began to ponder the prospect of all the beautiful girls I was going to meet by hanging around a winning football team. Unfortunately, my reverie was rudely interrupted when my two favorite brothers paid me a visit. Jim grabbed me by the collar and lifted me from the ground. "Close call, short stuff," he said.

"Hey, guys, calm down," I said, trying to calm myself down. "What are you complaining about? She won, and so did you. I told you before, it's in the bag."

"Yeah, well, it better be," Jim said.

"What are we doing here?" John interrupted. "We know this isn't going to work. Brandon's ideas never work. Flymow's already working us twice as hard, just because he's trying to prove something to him and Sarah. If we mess up and this doesn't work, we're dead. It's not worth the risk. I say we call the whole thing off, kick his brains in right now and save ourselves the hassle of doing it later."

"Whaaa!" I screamed.

I was well into saying my prayers when I got help from an unlikely source. "Hey, what are you bozos doing?" Sarah yelled. She ran up and grabbed Jim by the ear. "Get your hands off of him, chump," she said, twisting until Jim howled in pain and dropped me. "So, you guys can't live with the thought of me succeeding, is that it? Well, that just hacks me off. I'm your kicker, whether you like it or not. Flymow just told me I made the team. It's too late to call it quits now, so you'd better get your attitudes adjusted. Now, blow, or I'll have to get tough with you."

Jim grumbled a bit, but being a quarterback, he knew that even Timmy Nelson was capable of getting tough with him. He picked up his helmet and tapped John on the shoulder. "She's right. You saw Pritchard. We've got no choice."

"Yeah, I guess," John agreed reluctantly. He smiled at me. "I guess there's always time to whip your butt if it comes down to that." He picked up his helmet and followed Jim into the locker room.

"Gee, thanks, Sarah," I said. "You really saved my bacon."

"Can it, shrimp. The only reason I'm here is because Flymow told me to do the rookie run. Besides, you owe me twenty, and I want you in one piece so I can collect." She rolled her eyes to the heavens. "How did I ever get myself into this?" She picked up the water jug and glared at me. "You and your bright ideas."

"I thought it went rather well," I protested as we headed for the locker room. "In fact . . ."

I was cut off by the sound of heavy footsteps gaining on us. Sarah and I turned around to find Ferraro jogging to catch up. Dangling free from one hand was his helmet, which he grasped firmly by the face mask. His curly, black hair was matted down with sweat, and although fatigue creased his face, his eyes danced brightly as he looked at Sarah. "Hiya!" he called out.

Sarah turned back around, put her head down and picked up her pace as Ferraro trotted up beside her. She ignored him as we walked along. He leaned over and tried to catch her eye. "You know something? You're a pretty good football player for a girl."

When I heard that, I dove for cover. Sure enough, Sarah took the heavy, metal water jug and slammed it down right on top of Ferraro's foot, causing him to yelp and hop around like a circus clown.

"You know," Sarah said sarcastically, "you do a really good kangaroo imitation. For a boy." She snatched up the jug and marched off.

The pain eventually subsided enough for Ferraro to limp along after Sarah. When he caught up to her, he grabbed her elbow and spun her around. "You don't always have to be so aggressive!" he yelled.

Sarah rose a few inches. "Oh, yeah, what do you

know about it? When was the last time you were treated like a big joke? You don't think I didn't notice the way all the guys acted back there when I was kicking with Pritchard? So, tell me, Ferraro, who's side were you on?" Her eyes narrowed into an icy stare. "If I didn't stick it to you guys every chance I got, you'd eat me for lunch." She took a deep breath, the muscles of her face slackened, her whole body appeared to shrug. "And I was dumb enough to think that maybe this time things would be different."

Ferraro didn't follow when Sarah stalked off. He merely stood in place, his mouth hanging open. Poor guy, I think he had just fallen in love.

CHAPTER 5

The first day of school is generally a pretty exciting time for me. With all the new people, teachers and subjects surrounding me, I always feel a little like I do at Christmas time. You know, waiting and waiting in anticipation, wondering if that great-looking present under the tree contains a really neat gift or just socks and underwear.

That question was answered for me when, about five minutes into my first class, world history, the girl sitting in front of me spun around in her chair and merrily said, "Hi! I'm Janice Johnson! What's your name?"

I was in love before she'd even finished her first sentence. She was the most beautiful girl I'd ever seen. She had long, golden blond hair that draped gracefully down across her shoulders. Her slightly oval face and wonderfully high cheekbones were set off perfectly by the tiniest hint of an upturned nose. And her eyes! They were so blue that if you looked into them deeply enough, you could actually see through this universe and into the next.

In fact, she was so good-looking that I was sure she couldn't possibly have been talking to me. I quickly looked around the room, but no one else responded to her greeting, and when she thrust her hand across the desk at me, I knew there was no mistake. I took a deep breath, grabbed her hand and began to pump it furiously. "Hello," I heard myself say in a high-pitched squeak. "My name's Brandon Lewis."

"Pleased to meet you," she replied as our hands disengaged. "Lewis, Lewis . . ." she added, thinking. "You're not related to all those Lewises on the football team, are you?"

"Well, actually I am. I'm their brother."

"No kidding?" She leaned forward. "I think it's just great what your sister's doing, playing on the team and all. It's a real inspiration to the rest of us girls, having someone go out and prove it's possible to compete with the boys."

At this point, I wasn't above tying myself to

Sarah's exploits. "You know, that's the exact argument I used when I persuaded Sarah to try out for the team."

Janice's eyes widened. "It was your idea?"

"Sure. I'm no dummy. I want to be part of a championship team as much as anyone."

"So you play football, too?" she asked enthusiastically.

I almost went into shock. "Oh, gosh, no! Do I look crazy? You should see what those people do to themselves!"

"Well, I've seen them, and I think it's kind of heroic. I just love to watch football. That's why I became one of the cheerleaders this year."

Wow! A cheerleader! "You know," I said, leaning forward, "I'm not a football player, but I do play basketball."

"You do? Rad! So do I!"

"Really?" I took my eyes off her captivating face just long enough to give the rest of her a quick glance. Sure enough, I spotted a pair of fairly long legs tucked up underneath her desk. It hadn't occurred to me before, but she must've been at least five foot ten. She also possessed the slender, long arms and delicate, fine-boned hands that are frequently the hallmark of a basketball player. "Hey, that's great! We'll have to go out sometime and shoot some hoops together."

"Yeah, that'd be a lot of fun." Then, with a slightly wicked smile she added, "I'd just love to show you my double-clutch, gorilla dunk. It's max cool!" She gave me a wink, then turned back toward the front of the room, where Mr. Clark, our teacher, had begun his lecture.

Hmmm, something about the tone of her voice struck me as just a little strange. A double-clutch, gorilla dunk? Nah, couldn't be. Finally, I turned my attention to Mr. Clark, which was a big mistake, because for what seemed like the next two days he droned on and on about the Cradle of Civilization or some other such nonsense.

Eventually, the bell rang. I gathered up my books and sprinted out of the classroom only to find Janice waiting there.

"That was soooo boring!" she exclaimed, rolling her eyes toward the heavens. She motioned to me, and we began walking down the cement sidewalk toward the central hub of the campus. "What other classes do you have?" she asked.

I reached into my notebook and pulled out my schedule. She glanced over the list and suddenly her eyes lit up. "This is great! We've got math and Spanish together, too. How are you in math?"

"I'm pretty good," I answered cautiously. "I usually get A's."

"That's awesome! You can help me out with my

homework, then, because I'm just terrible."

She may not have realized it, but at that point I would've eaten her homework. Just then, the warning bell for the start of the next period sounded. "Whoops!" Janice cried out. "I've got to find my English class before I'm late. See you in math class!" she called over her shoulder as she took off running. "'Bye!"

I was frozen dead in my tracks as I watched her disappear around the corner. I didn't know what to think. I was elated. I was scared. She was too perfect. It had me worried.

But not for long because for the next few days all my attention was focused on the football team as they prepared for the first game of the season. It seemed as though Coach Knox had purposely laid out an obstacle course of responsibilities for me to traverse. There were boxes of game uniforms to sort out, charts and graphs to draw up, chalk lines and yard markers to be laid out on the football field. I could sense him testing me, so I carried out my assignments with fierce efficiency. The way the team was coming around, with Jim playing like Joe Montana, John and Ferraro blasting everything in sight and Sarah booming towering punts, there was no way I was going to allow myself to be perceived as a weak link.

Even Timmy Nelson had begun to contribute. Having taken Sarah's advice to heart, he'd rapidly turned into a terror on the special teams, seemingly always the first downfield to make the tackle on punts and kickoffs. It drove Coach Knox up the wall as Timmy dodged blockers, then tackled the ball carrier around the ankles. Although he screamed bloody murder every time he witnessed this cowardly act, there wasn't much he could do about it, because Timmy had progressed to the point where he never missed a tackle.

Leading up to that first game, Coach Knox gradually increased the intensity of practices until he had successfully created an atmosphere of unrestrained violence. By Thursday, practice resembled a series of brutal muggings, with cheap shots abounding. So many fights broke out that at times I'd have sworn I was in the middle of a mob trying to get tickets to a Rolling Stones concert. The team, as a whole, took on the appearance of a wounded animal, ready and eager to lash out at anything that dared cross its path. Individually, the players were so keyed up that they did strange things, like holding contests to see who could run into the goal post the hardest. When Coach Knox blew an end to that practice, he wore the tired smile of a man who knew he'd done all he could to prepare his team properly. The rest would be up to them.

Friday morning, I was up early putting on my fanciest rags. As you might expect, Coach Knox required his team to dress up on game days. Sneakers and jeans were definitely out. Slacks, dress shoes and ties were the order of the day. Some of the players grumbled about it, but I thought it was kind of cool, especially since I was greeted with approving stares throughout the day by girls who mistakenly thought I was one of the players.

During Spanish class that afternoon, Janice turned around and said, "You certainly do look nice today, Brandon."

Her smile sent a warm tremor rushing through my body. "Thanks. I wore it just for you. So tell me, do I look like a quarterback or a linebacker?"

She laughed. "Oh, don't be silly. You look like the water boy."

I put on my best indignant look. "I am not the water boy. I'm the team manager. It's a job that carries with it a great deal of responsibility."

"Oh? Really?" she said breezily, brushing aside my protest. Suddenly, her eyes lit up. "Now, your brother Jim, he looks like a quarterback. Did you see him today?" She rolled her eyes to the ceiling. "He's gorgeous! That brown shirt he's wearing makes his shoulders look even broader than . . ."

I cut her off. "Before you get any ideas about Jim, I think there's something you should know."

"What's that?"

"It's just that he's not . . . well, he's not normal."

"He's not?"

I flashed her a look of grave concern. "Yeah, it's something the family's been keeping secret for years. A medical problem. You see, Jim was born without a brain."

"Without a brain?!"

"Yep, I'm afraid so. The doctors couldn't believe it either. Said it was only the second time they'd ever seen something like that; my brother John was the first. I guess they've been talking about doing a transplant, but they can't find a brain that's small enough. They say even a baboon brain has about ten times more capacity than he could ever use."

As I spoke, Janice's face slowly dissolved into the slightly embarrassed smile of someone who knew she'd just been taken for a ride. "Very funny, Brandon." She set a look of mock sternness on her face, barely able to suppress a giggle that was trying to break through. "You certainly have an adolescent sense of humor."

"Hey, who's joking!" I protested. "He reads *National Lampoon* and thinks it's funny. He listens to Barry Manilow albums. He watches Rambo movies. Now, I ask you, does that sound like someone who's got a brain?"

That made her crack up completely, which in turn caused Mrs. Rodriguez, our teacher, to begin yelling at us in Spanish. I couldn't understand what she was saying because she hadn't yet taught us any Spanish swear words. Nonetheless, I caught the general drift of where she was coming from, so I slunk down in my seat and stayed there for the remainder of the period.

Well, the rest of the day just flew by, and before I knew it I found myself down in the locker room beginning final preparations for our game. As the players dressed, a tense and somber mood settled over the room. And rightfully so, because we were about to take the field against West Valley High. Now, West Valley had probably the biggest, ugliest, evilest-tempered group of animals ever assembled on the face of the earth, and that was just their cheerleaders. The guys on their team were so mean and nasty that I suspect most of them went straight to prison after graduating from high school before they even had a chance to commit a crime.

This was the school where the football players shaved their heads to set themselves apart from the rest of the student body. You'd think the fact that they all carried bicycle chains and switchblades would be enough, but not at West Valley High. It was one *bad* school.

Once everyone was finally dressed, I walked over to the girls' locker room to get Sarah. She was sitting on the bench, and I could see from the look in her eye that she'd been engaged in some serious psyching up. "How do you feel?" I asked.

"A little apprehensive . . . nervous, I guess," she said, as she stared balefully at the wall in front of her.

"Well, don't worry, you'll do just fine."

She looked up at me and nodded her head determinedly. "I know that." She jumped to her feet. "Let's go."

I turned, and she followed me back to the boys' locker room, where she sat down among the players and joined them in staring balefully at the wall in front of them. You could tell she was one heck of a player from the way she displayed that rare ability to stare balefully at any given wall at any given time.

The tension in the room was almost unbearable. I looked around and noticed Ferraro glaring intently at a picture that he had taped to his forearm. Suddenly, he rose to his feet.

"I cut this out of the newspaper," he said, pointing to his arm. "It's a picture of Willie Dupree. The article said that he's going to run all over us and that West Valley is going to kick our butts." He paused for a second to let that sink in. "Well, I don't know about any of you, but I don't intend to let anyone kick my butt." He began breathing harder, and a slightly deranged look appeared in his eyes. "You see this guy right here?" he asked, staring at the picture. "I'm not going to just hit him tonight, I'm going to punish him, I'm going to hurt him, I'm going to eat him up! Do you hear me, I'm going to eat him up!"

Everyone stared in wonderment as Ferraro reached down, viciously ripped the picture from his forearm and stuffed it into his mouth. A huge gasp arose when suddenly the picture vanished. In his excitement Ferraro had actually eaten it!

That was like throwing raw meat to the lions. The entire room erupted. My brother John jumped to his feet, jammed on his helmet and began slamming his head into the lockers. The rest of the team unleashed wild war cries as they threw their bodies into the walls and into one another. It was a pretty frightening display of pure animalistic fervor, and I pressed myself tightly against the door, hoping not to be picked off by a stray, careening body. Just then the door flew open. I went stumbling out backward and crashed heavily into the wall across the hall.

Coach Knox, who'd opened the door, stared down at me in disgust. "Quit fooling around, son. Can't you see we've got some important business to attend to?"

He turned back around. A huge grin spread across his face as he viewed the chaos inside. He stepped in, waited for a moment, then raised his hand, which instantly caused the players to sit down and fall silent, except for the few who continued to wheeze and drool.

"Well, gentlemen . . ." Just then his gaze fell upon Sarah and he flinched. Squaring his jaw he hastily moved on. "Uh, as I was saying, in a few short minutes you will all walk out onto that field and go to war. That's exactly what it is, gentlemen, a war. The stakes are high. To the victor goes self-respect. The loser will leave in disgrace, forced to answer some very harsh questions concerning the quality of his character." The fire that sparked in his eyes let everyone know which side of the fence he intended to finish on.

"Now, a lot of things go into winning that war, gentlemen, but most of all it takes pride and dedication. It's the pride that makes you give twice as much effort as you've got to give. It's the dedication that pushes you beyond what is possible, so that every time you get hit, you hit back even harder, so that you dig even deeper when you find the well is dry, so that you continue to drag yourself up and down that field out there even when you think you have nothing left to give!" His words echoed through the room, and I could tell that the players were completely entranced, because they all wore the same glassy-eyed look that you often see at a Grateful Dead concert.

Coach Knox looked up and down the bench, making solid eye contact along the way. "Tonight, you have the chance to test the outer limits of your courage and your desire. I have only one question. Are you ready to meet that challenge?"

The players jumped to their feet. "Yes, sir!"

"Who's going to show the most courage . . ."

"We are!"

". . . the most desire . . ."

"We are!"

". . . the most dedication that this state has ever seen?"

"WE ARE!!!"

"Well, then, gentlemen, I suggest we go out and kick some butt!"

Amid a deafening roar, the team exploded toward the door. Unfortunately, Timmy Nelson, who had been sitting at the end of the bench with his eyes blazing, became the shell that was fired from the cannon. I say unfortunately because I had closed the door behind me when I entered the room to hear Coach Knox's rousing speech and had not yet had the chance to reopen it. That didn't seem to matter to Timmy because he ran headfirst into it. He went down like a shot, and I had to move quickly to pull his limp body out of the way and throw open the door before he was trampled to death by the wild stampede of players.

I leaned him up against the lockers, raced over to the first-aid kit and grabbed some smelling salts. I broke them open and thrust them under his nose. Slowly, he came to. His eyes, which were spinning counterclockwise, began to slow down. Finally, they stopped, but then started up again, only this time clockwise. I figured that must mean he was okay, so

I grabbed him by the shoulder pads and hoisted him back to his feet. I gave him a big slap on the back as he charged out the door to rejoin the team. Who knows, maybe his father was right. Maybe all this craziness really would make a man out of him.

CHAPTER 6

Once everyone had departed from the locker room, I took a moment to catch my breath. Having spent my entire life around football players I was aware that they were a little different, but it wasn't until just then that I realized exactly how dangerous and demented they really were. Why, I'll bet if they were to round up all the football players in the country, stick copper wires up their noses, then lock them together in one big room, there wouldn't be any need for nuclear power plants.

I gathered up the equipment and staggered out to the field. Both teams were well into their pregame warm-up. I walked over to the sideline and looked up into the stands. The place was packed.

As I removed some ice packs from the first-aid kit, I heard someone call out my name. I looked over, and there, on the track that encircled the football field, stood Janice, along with the other cheerleaders. Her slender, long legs rose gracefully up from her white sneakers and disappeared beneath her blue woolen skirt at midthigh. She looked adorable in the snug, gold sweater that completed the other half of our school colors. I smiled and gave her the thumbs-up sign, which prompted the other cheerleaders to oooh and aaah while playfully jabbing her in the side. Her face turned beet-red, and I'm sure mine did as well. With a sheepish grin she gave one more little wave, then turned to join the others in the start of a routine.

Out in the middle of the field, the captains met and the coin was flipped. West Valley won the toss and elected to receive. The crowd rose to its feet as our kickoff team took the field. It roared as Sarah began her sprint toward the ball. The roar increased in volume and reached a crescendo at exactly the instant she made contact. The ball rose in a high, lazy arc and descended into Willie Dupree's arms at the goal line.

Willie took two quick, short steps to the left, then suddenly cut back toward the right sideline, breaking open and looking as though he might run for quite some distance. Then, suddenly, came Timmy Nelson, slicing between blockers and diving toward Willie. This caught Willie by surprise, and he shifted into a fancy little stutter step, designed to make Timmy miss. He didn't realize it, but miss is exactly what Timmy had intended to do all along. Willie froze as Timmy landed at his feet, grabbed his ankles, then flipped him to the ground at the twenty-yard line.

The players along our sideline went wild. Willie was not quite so happy. He slammed the ball to the ground in disgust, scrambled to his feet, then reached down and pulled Timmy up by the front of his jersey. "What kind of tackle is that, you little wimp?" he screamed in Timmy's face. "You're supposed to stick your head into my numbers!"

"That's what I've been telling him all along," Coach Knox mumbled, looking slightly embarrassed along the sideline.

"That's just the way I tackle," Timmy said meekly.

Willie was not appeased. "What are you trying to do, man, make me look bad in front of all my girl-friends?"

Timmy was taken aback. "No, of course not!"

"Listen, chump," Willie continued. "I've spent years workin' on my moves, and I got 'em all. I can juke, I can stutter-step, I can shuffle, I can glide. I can do a three-sixty spin. But I ain't never played against nobody who missed me on purpose, then grabbed my

74

ankles, so I ain't got no move for it." He pulled Timmy forward until their face masks met. "The stands are full of college scouts tonight, and they're all lookin' at me. They want to see a little magic, so you'd better try and hit me next time or I'll rip your scrawny little head off! You hear me?"

"Uh, uh . . . yes, sir," Timmy said as he backed away.

Timmy was still shaking his head in confusion when he got to the sideline. Ferraro stepped forward and snapped on his chin strap. "C'mon, D, let's go hit somebody!" he shouted as he led the defense onto the field.

West Valley began its offensive series with two running plays up the middle. This resulted in a couple of massive pileups and very few yards gained. On third down, their quarterback dropped back. Crozier, who was playing defensive end, looped to the inside and broke through the center of the line. The quarterback cocked his arm, ready to throw, which caused Crozier to jump into the air and fling his arms up in hopes of deflecting the ball.

It didn't take more than an instant for the smell to hit the quarterback. His face turned green, and he staggered sideways a few steps and treated us to a full pirouette before crashing face-first into the turf. The referee's whistle blew. Fourth down.

As the West Valley players helped their stunned

quarterback from the field and their punting unit ran on, fingers were pointed, profanities hurled and threats issued over our team's "dirty" tricks. They were lucky Crozier hadn't burped. That would've wiped out their entire sideline as well.

West Valley punted, and we took over on our own twenty. Since Coach Knox sent in all the plays, it was not surprising that our offense started out extremely conservative.

On first down, Leroy ran off tackle and smack into the West Valley middle linebacker, who twirled him in the air like a baton, then dumped him on his head. This did not deter Coach Knox in the least. On the next play, he ordered a sweep around left end. The defense reacted immediately and strung the play out along the line of scrimmage. Leroy had little alternative but to head straight out of bounds, a prospect that didn't seem to greatly upset him, considering the pack of ferocious animals that were in hot pursuit of his body.

On third down, Leroy was once again sent up the middle. This time a defensive lineman grabbed one of his legs while a linebacker latched onto the other. The two of them then played a rather spirited game of make-a-wish and were within inches of insuring that Leroy never fathered children when the referees blew their whistles.

All that "jamming" of the ball had resulted in a

paltry four yards gained, so we had to punt. As our offense came off the field, Leroy limped over to Jim. "Why don't you give the ball to someone else? I'm getting *killed* out there!"

Our punting team quickly lined up, and when Sarah received the snap from center she unleashed a monster kick. The punt sent Willie Dupree back-pedaling furiously, but to no avail. The ball dropped in over his head, hit the five-yard line and bounced straight out of bounds. The crowd roared. It was the perfect "coffin corner" kick.

Unfortunately, Sarah never got the chance to see the end result of her effort. While her leg was still fully extended skyward, Horace Broadnax, one of the most vile and evil players to ever set foot on the face of the earth, charged in and buried his shoulder pad into her ribs, sending her tumbling head over heels.

If he thought that was going to intimidate Sarah, he was sadly mistaken, because she immediately scrambled to her feet and sprinted over to where he stood. She ripped the helmet from her head. "What do you think you're doing, you bozo?" she screamed into his face.

Horace's eyes popped out at the sight of Sarah's long, red hair. He turned to his sideline and yelled, "Hey, guys, look at this! They're so hard up, they've got to use girls on this team!" Their entire team broke up laughing. Horace turned to Ferraro, who had been blocking for Sarah. "Hey, Ferraro," he sneered, "do you wear a dress during practice too?"

Ferraro lunged forward and grabbed Horace by the throat. The referee and Sarah got there just in time to prevent him from removing Horace's head and donating it to the primate section of the Smithsonian Institution.

The ref wedged himself between them, while Sarah climbed Ferraro's back and pulled him away. "C'mon!" she yelled in his ear. "Forget it! This bozo's not worth skinning your knuckles on!"

"I'm going to kill him!!" Ferraro screamed.

"Don't be an idiot," Sarah said, separating him further from Horace. "That's exactly what he wants you to do, start a fight and get kicked out. Do your talking on the field!"

Ferraro spun around. He and Sarah stood and glared at one another for a moment. Finally, Ferraro muttered a few choice words and ran over to join the defense. He began to play like a man possessed. He was everywhere, sacking the quarterback, knocking down passes and laying waste the entire West Valley offense. The way they began carrying West Valley players from the field, I was worried that they might run out of stretchers.

Despite Ferraro's inspired playing, the best our team could do was perpetrate a stalemate. Both teams did little more than tear up the middle of the field, and the half ended at 0-0.

The locker room at halftime was a pathetic sight. Moans and groans filled the room. There was blood everywhere. Bodies were strewn all over the place, sprawled out on the floor, stretched across benches, propped up against the lockers.

I set to work. To some, I gave smelling salts. For others, I bandaged their wounds as best I could. A few were beyond help, so I did a quick sign of the cross over their prone bodies and moved on.

Coach Knox walked into the room and surveyed the carnage. "Well, gentlemen," he began, not looking all that displeased by what he saw. "It's been a war, a good, hard-fought war, for one half now. You've shown great courage by not allowing the enemy to advance into the end zone. But this half, you'll be called on to accomplish much more. You're going to have to break through the enemy's line of defense, and keep breaking through, until we have broken his spirit and advanced into the land of six points. It won't be easy, nothing worth fighting for ever is. But if you're willing to give more than you've ever given before, gentlemen, then we will be victorious."

I don't know what came over me at that moment, but I couldn't help leaning over to Timmy Nelson and saying, "You know, things would go a whole lot better if he'd just open things up a little on offense."

"WHAT IN THE HECK'S GOING ON OVER THERE, BRANDON!?" Coach Knox's voice boomed through the locker room. "If you've got something to say, then say it to all of us."

I froze in place. All eyes in the room turned in my direction. My brothers shook their heads in disgust and rolled their eyes to the ceiling. But Sarah seemed to understand what I was getting at. She gave me the thumbs-up sign.

I took a deep breath. "I said I think we should open it up a little."

"Open it up?" he asked, sounding as though he was unfamiliar with the concept.

"Well, uh, yeah. It just seemed to me that they've got all the big, burly guys and we've got all the athletes. If we'd just mix up our plays, go deep a few times . . ."

"Open it up?" Coach Knox repeated.

"Sure, I'll bet we could blow the out."

"ENOUGH!" Coach Knox looked me square in the eye. "What we are engaged in this evening, young man, is something you obviously know nothing about. This is a battle that men have been waging since they first picked up sticks and stones. It's a wonderful, glorious struggle, one that brings honor to all who participate in it. How dare you suggest that I turn something that pure into a cheap spectacle by, how did you put it, opening it up?"

"I'm not suggesting turning anything into a cheap spectacle," I protested. "I just think we should . . ."

"I said *enough!*" He stood up and turned to the team. "Each and every one of you has a job to do this half. Now, get out there and do it!"

Despite Coach Knox's impassioned plea, the second half went pretty much like the first, with some tremendous hitting and very little else. Then, with just a couple of minutes to go in the game, it happened, the break everyone had been waiting for, though not in the form one would normally expect. It occurred on a play where Leroy carried the ball and was hammered before he'd even had the chance to get back to the line of scrimmage.

As he lay stunned on the ground, Horace Broadnax stood over him and said, "C'mon, Leroy, run this way again. I want to beat on you just like your mama used to."

Leroy leaped to his feet and went face mask to face mask with Horace. "What was that, chump? Did you say somethin' 'bout my mama?"

Horace smiled. "Yeah, man, I said you look just like her and she looks like an orangutan."

It took about four players to pry Leroy's fingers from around Horace's throat. "Nobody talks to me like that, and I mean nobody!" Leroy yelled as he was forcibly dragged away. He looked up at John, who had him in a bear hug. "C'mon, big man, block for me. We're goin' down this field right now!"

On the very next play, John fired off the line and ran over Horace like a freight train. Leroy followed close behind, broke to the outside and took off down the sideline for a fifteen-yard gain that kept the drive alive.

From there on it was Leroy, Leroy and more Leroy. He ran ferociously behind John's superb blocking. There were no fancy moves or spins during that drive—Leroy simply ran right through anyone who got in his way. Each time, after being tackled, he dropped the ball on the head of the dazed tackler and said, "Talk 'bout *my* mama, chump," in an indignant huff, before storming back to the huddle.

The team systematically worked its way downfield. Unfortunately, the clock moved faster than the ball, and Jim was forced to call our last time-out with five seconds to go in the game and the ball resting on the West Valley ten-yard line. There was time for only one more play.

The team gathered around as Coach Knox decided on which final play to call. Just then, Sarah trotted over and barged into the discussion. "Well, here I am," she announced, "so let's put those three on the board and get out of here."

Coach Knox looked confused. "What are you talking about?"

"I'm talking about the winning field goal, Flymow.

Remember, I'm a kicker, so I'll just put this baby through and we can all go home happy, okay?"

"A field goal," Coach Knox said to himself. Then it sank in. "A field goal!" he howled, almost coming out of his shoes. "You don't think I'm going to allow *this* football game to be decided by a cheap little field goal, do you? Why, why, that would be dishonorable!"

"Aw, c'mon, Flymow," Sarah said. "There's nothing dishonorable about it. Look, you've screwed things up enough tonight with your play calling, so why don't you just let me kick the field goal and win this game?"

Jim cut in. "Uh . . . you know, Coach, I think she's right. There's no way she can miss from there."

Ferraro pushed his way into the group. "Don't listen to them, Coach. Run the ball. This game means too much to take a chance on a girl winning it with a field goal."

"Hey, fella, why don't you just butt out?" Sarah yelled at Ferraro.

Ferraro rose up to his full height. "Oh, yeah? Well, why don't you just be quiet? Nobody asked your opinion anyway."

John charged through the cluster of players and jammed his finger into Ferraro's chest. "Listen, buddy, don't you talk to my sister like that!"

Coach Knox looked around. Mayhem abounded as

the players argued among themselves.

"Kick!" shouted Sarah.

"Run!" shouted Ferraro.

Coach Knox just shook his head and walked over to where I was standing. "Well, son, what do you think?"

Oh boy! Just my luck. "Uh, I think whatever you decide on is probably the best thing."

Coach Knox was not satisfied. "Don't give me that garbage, son. You've been acting like an assistant coach from the minute you showed up around here. It's too late to back down now. It's time to put your money where your mouth is."

I swallowed hard. "Kick the field goal."

"Kick the field goal?"

"Yes, sir, kick the field goal."

Coach Knox gave me a long, hard stare, then turned and walked back to the mob that was still violently arguing away. "Kick the field goal," he said.

Everyone stopped and stared at him. "I said, kick the field goal!" he yelled.

The team went scurrying in a million different directions. The offensive unit hurried off the field, while the field goal team hurried on. Sarah snapped on her helmet and winked at me, then at Coach Knox. "Don't worry, Flymow, just think of it as artillery. They still use that in wars, don't they?"

As Sarah lined up for the kick, the West Valley players across the line began jumping up and down, waving their arms and yelling things so nasty that even Coach Knox blushed. None of this distracted Sarah, though. When the ball was snapped and spotted, she purposefully strode forward and, in classic soccer style, caught it flush on the inside of her foot, following through until her knee almost touched her chin. The ball rose quickly and easily cleared the outstretched hands of the desperate West Valley players. It continued upward, end over end, until it split the uprights and disappeared into the darkness, far beyond the track.

The referees threw their arms into the air, signaling the kick good, which touched off a wild celebration. The team charged out and mobbed Sarah, while the students in the stands charged out and mobbed the team. From the way everyone carried on, you'd have thought that we had just won the world championship. As the West Valley players watched in disbelief, the team lifted Sarah up on their shoulders and carried her off the field, with the entire stadium filing out close behind them.

I'd nearly made it all the way to the locker room before I realized that I'd left the bag of footballs and first-aid kit behind, so I hightailed it back to the field.

When I got there, I was surprised to find Coach Knox still there, sitting alone on a bench that moments earlier had held our second-string players. He stared at the goalposts with eyes that resembled misty marbles, and his head gently swayed from side to side. His mouth was moving, but I couldn't tell what he was saying. It wasn't until I'd picked up the equipment, circled behind the bench and quickly tiptoed by him that I finally heard his words.

"You and your bright ideas . . ." he repeated, over and over, ever so softly. "You and your bright ideas."

CHAPTER 7

"Wasn't that the most incredible game you've ever seen?" Janice's face was aglow Monday morning in world history class. "It's in all the papers. Sarah's a star!"

"Yeah, it was pretty exciting," I agreed, reliving those hours again in my mind, though I don't know why, because that game had already been relived, rehearsed and rehashed about one million times over the weekend around my house. Two lamps, one chair, a coffeepot and numerous dishes had become casualties of the reenactment of crucial runs, hits or kicks.

"I just loved the way she stepped in and kicked that winning field goal," Janice went on. "She was so in control, why, it was positively inspirational." She leaned forward. "You know, Brandon, the word is out that you talked Coach Knox into letting her do it. That was really a brave thing to do."

"Oh, I don't think I deserve all that much credit," I said, though I probably did. "Coach Knox had already come to the cliff. He just needed someone to push him off."

Janice's eyes continued to sparkle. "Well, I don't care what you say, I think what you did was very courageous, and it makes me feel good to know that there'll be someone like you around when I try out for the varsity basketball team."

". . ." I tried to speak, but no words came out.

"Brandon?"

I could feel myself losing control, but I resolved to remain calm. I knew there was a proper way to handle the situation, so I opened my mouth and gave it another shot.

"WHAT!?"

Every head in the room turned in our direction. Janice looked a little puzzled by my outburst. "Well, yeah," she said. "I've been thinking about it for quite a while, but watching your sister Friday night convinced me."

"But you can't do that!" Even as the words were

leaving my mouth, I knew I was blowing it, because for the first time in my life, my voice sounded exactly like Michael Jackson's.

Janice's eyes narrowed. "Why can't I?"

"Well . . . uh . . . because . . . because . . . you're a cheerleader!"

She stiffened in her chair. "Oh, I get it. It's okay to have a girl around as long as you're the one calling the shots. I . . . I don't believe it. You're nothing but a male chauvinist!"

With a huff, she spun around in her seat and rejoined Mr. Clark, who was in the middle of a boring old lecture about some Greek guy named Plate or Pluto or something like that.

I slumped down in my seat. I was totally blown away. Janice, a varsity basketball player? It just didn't seem real. I mean, Sarah was a jock, she's always been that way. Janice seemed different. I envisioned her jumping up and down, waving her pompoms and *leading* the cheers for me. I couldn't imagine her out there *with* me, sweating, getting elbowed in the face and diving for loose balls.

My head was swimming. I wondered if this was what they meant by betwixt and between. The more I thought about it, the more confused I became, so I finally put my head down on my desk and went to sleep, like everyone in the class had already done.

For the rest of the day, Janice froze me out. Every

time we saw one another she nodded politely and said hello, but that was it. No smile, no gossip, no chitchat, no nothing. It really made me look forward to football practice that afternoon. I was hoping that there'd be plenty of blood and guts. There's nothing like watching someone else's misery to make you forget your own.

That afternoon, misery became the operative word. It began innocently enough. I was watching the team warm up, with John and Ferraro leading the way, when I was hit by this really bright idea. "You know," I thought, "this team would really be complete if we just had someone like Timmy up there as a captain, too!"

Unfortunately, I was thinking out loud and standing right next to Coach Knox while doing it. He lit up like a Roman candle. "What did you say?"

A voice rang out. "He's right, Flymow. How about it?"

Coach Knox spun around and found himself staring at Sarah's sweet face. "Yeah," she went on, "considering who won the game for you Friday night, I think it's time we had a special teams captain."

Coach Knox stormed over and just about climbed into Sarah's face mask. "Winning games isn't good enough for you, Foots? You want to take over the whole team, too? Is that it?"

"What are you babbling about?" Sarah said angrily. "I don't want to take over the team, I just want you to make Timmy a team captain."

Coach Knox turned white as a sheet and fired a jaundiced look at Timmy. "Him . . . him!? Let a wimp be a captain on my team? Are you out of your mind?"

Sarah shook her head in disgust. "Come on, Flymow. Timmy's earned it. He works harder than anyone on this team. You know, you're always talking about pride and dedication . . . well, here's a chance to put your money where your mouth is."

"But, he's a cowardly ankle tackler!"

"That doesn't matter! All that counts is that he makes the plays and gets the job done."

Right about then, the only play Timmy could've made was pulling up worms with his teeth, because while Sarah and Coach Knox argued, he slunk down to the ground and slithered away on his stomach. He quickly wound his way among the players, like a snake, until he slid in behind John, whose massive frame temporarily shielded him from the battle going on upfield.

By this time, Coach Knox was so close to Sarah that his nose had disappeared inside her face mask. "I've heard just about enough out of you, Foots! You've had your fun, most of it at my expense, but this time you've gone too far!"

"But . . ."

"ENOUGH! I don't want to hear another word

out of you, not another peep! From now on, we're doing it my way, do you hear, my way!" All sweaty and red-faced, he turned toward the rest of the team. "Everyone, ON THE GOAL LINE!"

Things got brutal in a hurry. Forty-yard sprints, Burma Roads, you name it, they did it. By the time Coach Knox's fury was totally spent, bodies were littered across the field like horribly twisted rag dolls.

That must've been what Coach Knox had in mind, because as he surveyed the carnage, a smile came to his face.

"Congratulations," he announced. "Today, you've taken a major step toward becoming a great football team. Remember, greatness comes when we learn from our mistakes and build upon them. It comes when, rather than being satisfied with what we've already accomplished, we push ahead and strive to become even better. Now, I hope in the future you will all display a little more maturity and realize that success requires us to work that much harder to achieve the perfection that is the essence of this game. Is that understood?"

"OOHHH! . . . UUUH . . . OOOWW!" was the response as the players rolled around in agony.

"Good!" Coach Knox looked out across the horizon. The sun was beginning to sink. His eyes glazed over. "God help me, but I love it!" he shouted. "I love the smell of football in the afternoon!" With that, he sprinted off the field and over to the obstacle course, where he launched himself headfirst into the ten-foot-high barrier wall.

It took a few minutes, but eventually the players climbed to their feet and straggled toward the locker room. I gathered up all the equipment and headed in myself. As I staggered along under my cumbersome load, I looked up and found that Sarah was just a few yards ahead of me. I quickened my pace in the hope that maybe I could dump some of my garbage off on her, but before I could get there, Ferraro came trotting by, gave me a wink and fell in beside her.

"Hi!" Ferraro said. The lines of fatigue melted from his face as he smiled brightly.

Sarah looked up. The lines of fatigue on her face grew even deeper. "Hello," she said flatly.

They walked along in silence for a moment or two. "Pretty tough practice, huh?" Ferraro commented, trying to break the ice.

"I've seen worse."

"Yeah," he went on, "that sure made old Fly-mow . . . I mean Coach Knox . . . mad when you told him you wanted Timmy to be a team captain."

"Don't you start on me too!" Sarah erupted. "Timmy has a perfect right to be a captain . . ."

Ferraro threw up his hands. "Whoa, settle down, tiger! I'm not sure I like the idea of Timmy being a captain, but I think you're right; someone from the special teams deserves to be."

Sarah looked a little surprised. "Really?"

Ferraro cocked his head like he was considering something. "Timmy is a wimp, but on the other hand he always gets the job done. I guess that's really the bottom line, isn't it?"

"I always thought so."

Ferraro gave Sarah a long look. "Okay, I'll go along with it." He smiled. "It's not like I've never been wrong before, right? And I'll tell you what, I'll even put in a good word for him with the rest of the guys."

Sarah looked genuinely touched. "Well, gee, thanks, Ron. I really appreciate the support."

Ferraro gave her his best lady-killer grin. "Don't mention it, babe. That's what I'm here for."

Sarah's eyes widened. "Boy, you never give up, do you? I think the least you could do for me is come up with some original lines for a change."

Ferraro blushed. "Well, I . . . uh . . . it's just that . . . uh . . ."

Sarah shook her head and began to chuckle. Ferraro gave up trying to explain himself, shrugged his shoulders and joined in, so that within seconds they were laughing heartily together.

"Hey, that was quite a game Friday night, huh?" Ferraro asked enthusiastically, once their laughter had subsided.

"Oh, I don't know," Sarah replied, with a gleam in her eye. "I guess it wasn't bad."

"Wasn't bad?" Ferraro exclaimed. "Wasn't bad?" He leaned over and nudged Sarah in the ribs. "Boy, you're sure hard to please! Why, that game had it all. Drama, excitement, intensity, hard hitting . . . especially hard hitting."

"You're right," Sarah agreed. "There was some real popping going on out there, and you were popping the hardest. You kept us in that game, Ron. You played very well."

You could've transported a herd of elephants across the grin that filled Ferraro's face. "Thanks," he said. "You didn't do too bad yourself. That was a great kick you made."

Sarah dismissed his comment with a wave of her hand. "It wasn't a great kick. It was a chip shot. It was routine."

"Yeah, well, what I meant was, it was a great kick under the circumstances. Who'd expect a girl to come out and be successful under that kind of pressure?"

Sarah's smile vanished. "What are you talking about, you dummy? My being a girl has nothing to do with it. The only pressure around here is the pressure on your brain when you try to think. I couldn't believe the way you freaked out on the sidelines like that."

Ferraro seemed taken aback by the sudden turn of

events. "I didn't freak out," he protested weakly. "I just didn't know if you could do the job."

"Of course I can do the job, you knucklehead!" she yelled. "I'm on the team, aren't I? You wouldn't have stood there and argued if it had been Pritchard or one of the other guys about to kick that field goal."

An expression of horror crept into Ferraro's face. He finally realized just what it was that had made Sarah so angry. "Aw, come on, give me a break. I didn't really mean anything by it. You think it's easy for me? I'm not used to playing football with a girl. I always thought that girls wound up as cheerleaders."

"Oh, I see, like Bouncing Betty, I suppose?" Sarah sneered. Bouncing Betty was the head cheerleader, who'd gotten her name from the fact that, when she walked, certain parts of her anatomy moved up and down like the San Andreas Fault. Sarah eyed him coldly. "Let's get something straight, buster. I am not Bouncing Betty!"

Ferraro looked her up and down a couple of times. "Well, that's obvious," he said sarcastically.

Smoke spewed from Sarah's ears. "What's that supposed to mean, chump?" she demanded.

"I don't know!" Ferraro yelled irritably. "Maybe it just means that it might do you some good if you were a little more like her!"

Sarah trembled with rage. "Why, why, you . . . "

She lunged forward and threw her forehead into Ferraro's, giving him a taste of his own medicine with a vicious "reverse sleeper" hit.

There was only one problem. Neither of them was wearing a helmet. That didn't seem to bother Sarah, though. She barely twitched as Ferraro tumbled to the ground like a giant redwood. While he rolled around in the dirt, trying to figure out what day, week, month, year and universe he was in, Sarah stalked off to the locker room.

As I walked by, Ferraro's eyes were beginning to come back into focus. "What did I do? What did I do?" he cried out to me.

I just shook my head. "You play with fire, you're bound to get burned," I told him as I continued on in.

That's about how it went for the rest of the week; a lot of people got burned by a lot of fires. Coach Knox continued to drill the team as though he were preparing for another assault on Iwo Jima. Sarah hammered Ferraro every chance she got. Janice was still freezing me out.

Fortunately, we were playing Central High, which had a terrible team, that Friday night, and a big win seemed just the ticket for getting everyone back on track again. Unfortunately, when game time finally rolled around, the big blowout that everyone eagerly anticipated never materialized. From the minute we kicked off to start the game, I could sense that we were in deep trouble. The team was clearly out of sync. There were missed blocks, missed tackles, fumbles, stumbles and just plain old confusion. Coach Knox compounded the problem by becoming increasingly conservative in his play selection. As a result, going into the fourth quarter the game was all knotted up at 7-7.

Just when it appeared that this thoroughly mediocre struggle might end in a tie, Central High coughed up the ball deep in its own territory. Our offense desperately struggled to punch the ball into the end zone before time ran out.

They didn't move quick enough. Jim was forced to burn our last time-out with the ball on the twelve-yard line and mere seconds remaining.

Jim trotted over to the sideline. "Well, Coach, what do you think?" he said with a sly grin.

Coach Knox was not smiling. In fact, he didn't even acknowledge Jim's question. He simply stared into the darkness far beyond the end zone and muttered, "God, no, not again. Please, not again."

Jim leaned over, grabbed Coach Knox by the shoulder and shook him. "Coach? Coach? Snap out of it, we need a decision."

Sarah sauntered over. "Well, Flymow, here I am to save your bacon. You know, you should be careful, this is starting to become a habit."

Coach Knox recoiled at the sight of Sarah's evil grin. "I don't believe it," he whimpered. "This can't be happening again."

"C'mon, Coach," Jim said impatiently. "What do you want us to do?"

Coach Knox began backing away. "I don't care what you do," he sputtered. "Do whatever you want. Just leave me alone, do you understand? Please, leave me alone!" The team watched in stunned silence as he continued to backpedal down the sideline toward the other end zone, babbling incoherently all the while.

"Well, that's great, just great!" Jim was disgusted. "What do we do now?"

Everyone turned and looked at me. I took a deep breath. "I guess we kick the field goal."

Ferraro stepped in. "Damn right we kick the field goal." He turned toward my sister. "C'mon, Sarah, win this baby for us."

Sarah was not the type you had to ask twice. Strapping on her helmet, she gave Ferraro kind of a funny look, then trotted onto the field. Seconds later, we all trotted off with our second victory of the season.

This time, however, there was no wild celebration in the locker room afterward. Everyone realized that we'd just squeaked by a team we should've beaten by a good thirty points. We'd been flat, with none of the spark or fire that sets apart the truly great teams. The state championship, which only a few short weeks ago had seemed so real and attainable, now felt as though it were locked away in a safe on the bottom of the ocean. And the most distressing thing of all was, I was fresh out of bright ideas.

CHAPTER 8

In the following two weeks it was more of the same; we played terrible football and barely squeaked by our next two opponents. The worse we played, the tighter Coach Knox turned the screw. The frustration level among the players grew until, almost overnight, the character of the team changed. They went from a confident, cohesive, mean, hitting machine to a group of petty, argumentative babies. Drills, plays and practice became increasingly lifeless and were punctuated with pushing, shoving, finger pointing and foul language. Fights broke out at the drop of a hat. Some of the players even began talking about Leroy's mother. It was not a pleasant situation.

Finally, one Monday, things came to a head in the middle of Coach Knox's famous "nut-buster" drill. The nut-buster is a wonderful little exercise where the players run in place as fast as they can. At the sound of the whistle they fling themselves facefirst onto the ground. The whistle blows once more and they jump to their feet, where they begin running in place again. It may not sound like much, but I've seen it turn many a player into a babbling jellyfish.

The team had been at it for about ten minutes, responding to a whistle that blew faster and faster. Soon, all you could see was a mass blur that kept popping up and down. Finally, Sarah jumped to her feet and stayed there while everyone dove to the ground again. "This is ridiculous!" Her words echoed across the field. "Just what are you doing, Flymow?"

Coach Knox lowered the whistle from his lips. "We're learning the value of hard work, Foots, that's what we're doing. You see, if we learn the value of hard work, then maybe we won't have any more displays like the one we witnessed last Friday night."

"Well, that's the dumbest thing I've ever heard." Sarah looked around at the players lying on the ground, gasping for air. "I'll tell you what, Fly-mow—you let me know when you decide to get back to playing football, okay?" Then, to everyone's amazement, she walked off the field.

"Yeah, I should've known that you'd be the first one to break, Foots!" Coach Knox yelled bitterly, as she crossed the sideline.

The entire team stood in stunned silence as Sarah made her way across the blacktop and into the girls' locker room. Coach Knox turned back around and glared. "Anyone else here care to go AWOL?"

There was no reply, but if looks could kill, Coach Knox would've been six feet under right then and there. He was a little taken aback by the searing looks he received. "I know it's not pleasant," he tried to explain, "but sometimes it's necessary to weed out those among us who are not mentally and physically strong. Remember, a chain is only as strong as its weakest link. After all . . ." He stopped abruptly. "Wait a minute, what in the world am I justifying myself for? I'm the coach!" He immediately began firing back some pretty nasty looks himself. "Everyone, on the goal line!" he hollered.

Once again it was a case of run 'em till they drop. And drop they did. In fact, the remainder of practice was so grueling that even Coach Knox had broken a sweat by the time he was through.

After practice, my two big, lovable brothers paid me a visit.

"Well, shrimp, what are you going to do about this?" Jim asked.

"About what?" I tried to play dumb, an almost impossible task in my case.

"About Sarah! About Coach Knox! About this whole mess you've gotten us into!"

"Wait a minute, guys, just mellow out," I said, backing up. "I don't know what you want from me— I'm just the water boy."

"The team manager," John insisted. "It's a job that carries with it a great deal of responsibility."

"I don't think you understand," Jim added. "You don't have a choice. We're your big brothers, remember? We know all your little secrets. You know how every year you tell Dad that the dog has eaten his *Sports Illustrated* swimsuit issue? Well, we know that those teeth marks are really yours. Need I go on?"

"That's not fair! I've done more than my share to help out already."

John shook his head in disgust. He slapped Jim on the arm. "Come on, let's go in. There's no sense wasting any more time on him."

"Yeah, you're right." Jim fixed his eyes on me. "I expected a little more from you, short stuff. I guess I was wrong."

They turned and headed off. With my head down I started for the locker room. My mind was a mass of conflicting emotions. I'd been sucked in way over my head. I had never intended to get this involved; not with Sarah, my brothers, Coach Knox or this football team. Probably not even with Janice, when you got right down to it. I was no longer in control of anything, it seemed. It kind of made me feel like I was the President or something.

I was depressed, so I did the only thing to do under the circumstances: I went over to my locker, pulled out a basketball and walked out behind the school, where I began shooting baskets.

It's probably not very well known, but shooting hoops is like a miracle drug; it's guaranteed to cure what ails you. As I started out shooting lay-ups and short bank shots, I could feel the healing force invade my body. In no time at all, I had worked my way into that mesmerizing rhythm that comes from bouncing and shooting a basketball.

I picked up the pace, moving farther and farther from the hoop, until I was firing from way outside, at all sorts of weird angles, while nailing shot after shot. At that point the hypnotic effect of the sport took full control and I crossed the boundary into another universe, one where I became Michael Jordan, The Magic Man, Kareem and The Bird, all rolled into one. I found myself pulling down about two million dollars a year, while winning every game I played in with an assortment of last-second, off-balance, spectacularly spectacular jump shots. If that weren't enough, every beautiful woman in the world was madly in love with me.

Unfortunately, it is true that all good things must come to an end. Mine did when I heard a sweet, feminine voice call out, "Hey, shrimp, whatcha doing?"

Sarah walked over to where I was playing, grabbed the ball away from me and tossed up a twenty-five-foot hook shot. It went through so cleanly that the net barely rippled. She shook her head. "Why they pay those tall freaks all that money to do something so simple I'll never understand," she said.

"Maybe it's because it takes more than one lucky shot to be good at this sport, unlike some others I can think of!" I yelled over my shoulder while retrieving the ball. I silently thanked the heavens that basketball was one sport she'd never seriously taken up. "Anyway, what are you still hanging around this place for? You should've been out of here hours ago."

Sarah shrugged. "Oh, I don't know. I got into that shower and didn't feel like ever coming out again. Then I just sat on the bench in front of my locker and started thinking."

"What were you thinking about?"

"I was thinking that maybe I shouldn't have walked out on the team like that." She grabbed the ball from me and swished another twenty-five-footer. "But I'm sick of this. Flymow's ruining our whole season, and everyone out there blames me for it because they know he's trying to prove a point. He wanted to chase me out so he could have his football team back to himself. Well, fine. He can have it." By this time, Sarah had worked herself up to a look of steely resolve, but that suddenly dissolved as doubt crept in. "I don't think what I did was unreasonable. Do you?"

I turned the basketball over in my hands and stared at the seams. "I don't know. I guess that depends on why you came out in the first place."

"It wasn't my idea," she protested. "Remember the way you . . ."

"Come on, Sarah, give me a break. What's the real reason you came out?"

She thought for a moment. "I guess I just wanted to see if I could do it."

"Well, you've done it, you've shown them all. You've read the papers, you've heard the talk. This county's never seen anything like you. You've got serious talent, Sarah. Don't quit now, when you're so close to something special. With you, this team *could* win the state title."

Sarah chewed on her bottom lip. Her body sagged. "Why can't I just be like everyone else?"

I took my ball, spun it on my finger and stared at the blur. "I guess it's 'cause you're not like everyone else."

She looked out in the direction of the football field. "Well, maybe you are right." She sighed. "But I don't think I can put up with much more of Flymow's garbage."

I began dribbling the ball. The rhythm seemed to take over; something began whirling in my brain. Suddenly, I knew what had to be done.

"Don't worry," I told Sarah. "You just show up for practice. I'll take care of Coach Knox."

I scooped up the ball off the dribble, spun around and threw up a jump shot from about thirty feet. I caught nothing but the bottom of the net.

Sarah rolled her eyes. "Talk about lucky," she said.

"No, that one was pure skill," I replied. "Let's go home."

CHAPTER 9

On Tuesday I was up at the crack of dawn. I had to get down to the school to help Coach Knox grade the films from our previous game. Grading films is a little exercise where the coach reviews the game films and assigns a grade (A through F) to every player on every play. The grade depends on the manner in which each player has carried out his assignment on that particular play. At the end of the films, all the grades are averaged out and the player receives a game grade.

To give you some idea of what I'm talking about, Coach Knox's idea of an A performance goes something like this: As soon as the ball is snapped, you hurdle two or three opposition players, then slam into a fourth with sufficient momentum to break his ribs. Tossing that player aside, you rapidly move downfield and encounter another opponent. This time you lower your head and hit him so hard that his helmet shatters. As he's going down, you reach over and rip out his eyeballs, quickly eating them to give you the energy to take on the remaining six opposition players, which you do, leaving their broken bodies scattered across the field. After that, you run over and launch yourself into their bench, where, amid flying teeth, hair, football equipment and assorted other body parts, you send them all limping and crawling toward the nearest emergency room. Next, you climb up into the stands and proceed to clean out their entire rooting section. After you've pummeled and maimed a sizable portion of them, you hop on their team bus and drive straight to their home town, where you begin pillaging and plundering every man, woman, child, animal, house, tree and rock you can find until, when you're through, the place looks like ground zero after a nuclear attack.

That was what Coach Knox expected out of his quarterback, so you can imagine what sort of effort it took for anyone else on the team to get an A. In fact, the only guy who ever got an A from Coach Knox is presently doing twenty to life in the state pen.

When I arrived at Coach Knox's office, he was already in the process of threading the film through the projector. He looked tired, really tired. I could hardly believe my eyes. I mean, we're talking about a guy who doesn't like marathons because "they're not long enough."

Something was definitely up, something, I sensed, that might not be totally undesirable. Content to bide my time, I sat down in silence and picked up the ledger containing the names of the players and waited for Coach Knox to begin passing judgment. As the film began to roll, so did he.

"John Lewis!" he yelled, as though John were in the room with us. "What kind of fire-out block is that? No wonder the play only gained two yards. That's pitiful, that's pathetic, that's a C in my book." I dutifully wrote a C next to John's name.

"Look at Leroy!" Coach Knox screeched on the next play. "He looks like he's tiptoeing through a field of tulips! You've got to run hard in this game, son, run like you mean it. Give him a D."

The film continued on, with Coach Knox flipping the forward and reverse buttons on the projector back and forth, running and rerunning each play about a hundred times. He kept up a nonstop commentary all the while.

"No, no, Crozier! It's your job to contain that end sweep. You were lucky the smell got to that ball carrier when it did; otherwise he'd still be running down that sideline. Give him a C.

"What kind of hit is that, Pritchard? For crying out loud, you tackle like a punter! D!

"Ferraro! Don't rip the quarterback's head off when he doesn't have the ball! That's a D. No, wait a minute. On second thought, that's not such a bad idea. Give him a C instead."

Then, while we were watching Leroy get piled up along the sideline, Coach Knox suddenly bolted upright, out of his chair. "What is Nelson doing?" he demanded. He quickly rewound the film and ran the play over again. In the corner of the picture, Timmy was standing along our sideline with his back to the action, his gaze intently fixed on Bouncing Betty as she went through her famous "earthmover" routine.

"I don't believe it!" Coach Knox screamed. "He's not even paying attention to what's going on out on the field! Give him an F!"

"But, Coach, he wasn't even in the game," I protested.

"I don't give a darn!! Give him an F!" He flopped back down into his chair. "And you want me to make him a team captain. How can you make a team captain out of someone who spends half the game watching the cheerleaders?"

It went on like that for a while, but by the time we were into the second reel of the game, Coach Knox had become less animated. He continued winding down until, finally, he just sat in his chair, totally motionless, with his eyes riveted to the screen. The only sound in the room was the clicking of the projector as it continued to spit out the plays.

"Look at that," he muttered quietly, motioning toward the screen. "Just look at that. There's no life out there. There's no fire in their eyes. I've busted my rear trying to instill the proper qualities in this team, and it's as though they never listened to a word I said." He leaned forward and flicked the projector off. "You know, son, there was a time when I thought this was the best football team I'd ever seen, when I was sure that this would be the one to bring me that state championship. But now, I don't know, I just don't know."

It was a pretty sorry sight. But it cheered me up enormously. I'd been presented with the perfect opportunity. I made my move. "Maybe the problem is that nobody's having any fun, Coach," I said.

Boy, that perked him right up. "Fun!" he snarled, rising in his seat. "Fun? What are you talking about, son? This isn't badminton, this is football! It's not supposed to be fun!"

"But maybe it should be, Coach. Think about it. You've got everyone on such a short leash that the only thing they can do is get frustrated. If you'd just open things up a little, maybe you'd see that spark you're looking for."

"Open it up, open it up. That's all I ever hear anymore. You know, son, you're beginning to sound like a broken record, and that's not good. If you ask me, I think this team's afraid of hard work."

"It is not! Those guys have given you one hundred and ten percent from the very first practice. I think it's time for you to give a little in return."

"I suppose they have worked hard on occasion," Coach Knox reluctantly conceded. "But I was taught to play football one way: tough, no nonsense, straight ahead."

"Maybe times are just changing, Coach."

"I'll say they are!" He sounded disgusted. "First I have to put up with ankle tacklers, then with girls kicking winning field goals, and now you want to have fun, too? Well, I don't like it. No, sir, I don't like it one bit."

"But, Coach, if you don't lighten up some you're going to lose control of the team."

"Lose control! Lose control? I NEVER LOSE CONTROL!" he roared as he sent everything on his desk flying across the room with one angry sweep of his arm. "You know, ever since you and that sister of yours showed up, everyone around here wants to tell me what to do! I'm getting tired of it! Do you understand?"

I'd come too far to back down now. I stuck out my

chin defiantly. "Well, someone needs to straighten you out. At the rate you're going, this season will be ruined for everyone." I reached over and hastily gathered up my books. "Now, if you'll excuse me, I've got to get to class." I stood up and marched to the door.

"Just a minute there, son!" Coach Knox's voice boomed as I grabbed the doorknob. I spun back around and met his angry glare with one of my own.

Suddenly, his face softened. He pressed his eyes shut and took a deep breath. "What am I doing? I don't know what's come over me." He opened his eyes. "I'm sorry, son, I had no right to yell at you like that. You've done a fine job for me this year. You're just about the best right-hand man I've ever had." He closely scrutinized me while rocking back and forth in his chair. "In fact, now that I think about it, you'd make one heck of a Marine!"

"Gee, thanks, Coach," I said, trying my best to keep from throwing up. "But if you don't mind, I'd just as soon stick to basketball."

Coach Knox looked disappointed, and a bittersweet smile came to his face. "You do that, son," he sighed, "you do that." He turned around and flipped the projector on again. "For crying out loud, Pritchard!" he bellowed, picking up where he'd left off earlier. "How did I ever get talked into letting a punter become a defensive back?"

I left and hurried across campus. My heart was still

pounding and my knees felt rubbery as I took my seat in world history class. The die had been cast. Now, only time would tell.

All of a sudden, my nose began twitching. Janice was wearing some kind of perfume that made her smell like a bouquet of spring flowers. I sat there and took it all in, allowing my mind to wander. I was on the verge of a really good fantasy when I remembered that I'm allergic to spring flowers, so I did what I always do when that season rolls around. I began sneezing uncontrollably.

"Are you all right, Brandon?" Janice turned and asked after about the sixth or seventh time I'd sprayed her back.

"Yeah, yeah, I'm fine," I answered, once my eyes had cleared and my nose ceased its Mount Saint Helens imitation. "Boy, you sure affect me in wonderful ways."

Well, Janice didn't blink, she didn't frown, she didn't even crack a smile. She was one hard woman. "I'd love to chat, Brandon," she said, in the same polite, stiff voice I'd been getting for the last week and a half, "but I've got to take notes on this lecture. So, if you'll excuse me . . ."

By now I was down on my knees. "Come on, Janice. You haven't talked to me for days. You can't stay mad at me forever. Can you?"

A flicker of amusement flashed through her eyes,

but she suppressed it immediately. "Shhh, Brandon," she scolded. "What are you doing? Everyone's starting to stare at us. Get back in your desk and pay attention. This is a very important lecture."

I wanted to press my case further, but decided to drop the subject when I noticed Mr. Clark staring at me as though he wished capital punishment were legal in the classroom.

I climbed back into my chair and slunk down as far as I could go. It occurred to me that Janice was the one who'd make one heck of a Marine, and I figured that if she kept acting this way, I could always take my revenge by pointing her out to Coach Knox.

Later that afternoon, when practice time rolled around, I quickly gathered up my things and headed out to the field. I had earlier tilled the soil; now it was time to plant the seed and let nature take its course. When I got to the sideline, I called Leroy over.

"Say, Leroy, I'm really sorry about your mother," I said as I patted him gently on the back.

Leroy spun away. "What about her?"

"Well, Ferraro said . . ." I leaned forward and whispered in his ear.

His eyes widened, and he stepped back. "Ferraro said that?" he asked as he shot a glance out to the middle of the field.

"He sure did," I replied. "Sorry, Leroy."

"No problem," he said as he headed onto the field.

"Excuse me for a moment."

I watched as Leroy marched over to where Ferraro stood, grabbed him by the shoulder pad and spun him around. Leroy's finger shook in front of Ferraro's nose. Ferraro shrugged his shoulders. Leroy pointed over at me. Ferraro shrugged his shoulders. Leroy hauled off and slugged Ferraro right in the mouth. Ferraro did not shrug his shoulders.

"Why you son of a . . ." Ferraro screamed as he lunged forward at Leroy and threw a big, looping roundhouse punch.

Leroy was much too quick for that. He easily avoided the punch by taking a step back. This sent Ferraro flying sideways and his fist finally found its mark on John's jaw. The riot was on. Helmets, shoes, pads, fists: You name it, they were all flying through the air. Sarah punched Timmy, Timmy punched Leroy, Leroy punched Ferraro (again), Ferraro punched Crozier, Crozier punched John. It got so bad that even Jim punched someone. Of course, it was only a tackling dummy, but that was pretty good for him.

Unbeknownst to all these fighting fools, Coach Knox had made his way out to the field. Upon reaching the sideline, he stopped and stared unbelievingly at the chaos before him. "Don't worry, Coach," I yelled. "I don't think you've lost control of the team,

118

I think they've just decided to have a little fun on their own."

"I don't believe it," Coach Knox muttered. *"I don't believe it!* I've never seen anything like this in all my years of coaching!" He began rubbing his forehead with his fingers. He shot a sideward glance at me. "Well," he said, "you're the one with all the answers. What do you think?"

"I think there's only one thing left to do and you'd better do it in a hurry."

Coach Knox looked like he wanted to cry. "Do you really think so? Do I have to?"

"I'm sorry, Coach," I said sympathetically. "I'm afraid it's the only thing that'll save you now."

"Harmph!" he grumbled as he spun around and walked out to the field. He marched out into the middle of the fray and while bodies flew by, he fumbled for his whistle and, with trembling hands, managed to raise it to his lips. He blew a high-pitched scream that caused everyone to freeze in place.

"WHAT IN THE HECK IS GOING ON OUT HERE?!"

"He hit me!" the entire team responded in unison, with everyone pointing an accusing finger at everyone else.

Timmy pointed at Sarah. *"She* hit me!" he cried.

Coach Knox looked around in bewilderment. "Line up for calisthenics! NOW!"

The players mumbled and grumbled as they got into their respective lines. There were a few final shoves and some idle threats exchanged. Coach Knox looked over at me. He took a deep breath, then, grimacing, he yelled out, "Timmy Nelson, front and center!"

Timmy came slinking forward like a dog with its tail between its legs. "Y . . . Yes, sir?" he said meekly.

Coach Knox stared sourly at him for a moment, then his face went stone blank. "These guys," he said, motioning toward Jim and Ferraro, "obviously don't know what leadership means, so get up there and help them run this team through the exercises."

Timmy's eyes about popped out of his head. "Wha . . . ?"

"Don't just stand there, son! Get to it! Now!"

The team broke into shouts and laughter as Timmy sprinted to the front. "Way to go, Timmy!" "Atta boy!"

Coach Knox then marched over to Sarah. "Glad to have you back, Foots."

Sarah leaned back to study Coach Knox for a moment. Then, a smile slowly crept across her face. "It's good to be back, Flymow."

Coach Knox looked her over. "Okay, Foots, you've convinced me that you know how to kick, but tell me, do you know how to pass?"

Sarah just about fell over. "What!?"

"Never mind," Coach Knox said. "We'll get to that later." He clapped his hands together. "C'mon, c'mon, let's go!" he cried out to the team. "We've got a lot of work to do!"

The team positively flew through the rest of their exercises, and soon Coach Knox had everyone hopping as he introduced a whole assortment of new plays and formations, both offensive and defensive. There was something a little odd in his behavior, something I couldn't quite put my finger on. He carried this half smile on his face as he sprinted around the field, energetically explaining assignments and demonstrating techniques. There was something for everyone: stunts for the defensive linemen, end arounds, safety blitzes, long passes—the whole works. He covered so much ground that the practice lasted longer than any I'd ever seen. Funny thing was, nobody seemed to mind. The players looked like they were having a pretty good time, and some of them actually wore smiles as they left the field after practice ended. I was encouraged. It looked like my plan just might work. Now all we needed was a big win and we'd turn this thing around for sure.

CHAPTER 10

The next afternoon, I was out shooting hoops on the blacktop. Practice had gone well that day and I was feeling pretty good, so it didn't take long for me to get into a groove as I poured in one jumper after another in a wide arc around the key. I was right in the middle of winning yet another NBA championship with a seventh-game, twenty-foot buzzer-beater over Patrick Ewing when I spotted Janice walking across campus. In her loose-fitting, blue sweat suit and puke-green tennis shoes with fluorescent pink stripes, she looked for all the world as though she'd just stepped out of my dreams. Anxiety and confusion welled up inside. I just had to talk to her; the situation that existed between the two of us was eating me alive.

After nailing one more turnaround twenty-footer, I scooped up my ball and sprinted after her. "Hey, Janice," I yelled as I caught up to her, "what are you doing around here so late?"

Janice turned. "Oh, hi, Brandon. I just stopped by to pick up a few things I left in my locker. What are *you* doing?"

"Just getting in a little practice." I bounced the ball on the ground in front of me a few times. "Is it all right if I walk you home?" I asked.

She looked a little startled, then her face brightened a bit. "Sure, why not?"

We walked along in silence for a couple of blocks. Finally, I took a deep breath and said, "Hey, Janice, I'm really sorry about what I said to you that day in class."

"You are?"

"Well, yeah. I really didn't mean anything by it. I guess I just never thought of you like that before."

Her eyebrows shot up. "Like what?"

"You know, like a jock. It just sort of blew me away when you said you were going out for the varsity team."

Janice furrowed her brow. "I don't see why it should have. You obviously don't have a problem with your sister being on the varsity football team."

"That's just it. I've always thought of her as a jock. That's how she acts. You seem so different."

"But maybe we're really not so different."

"Huh?"

"Maybe I'm wrong, but I've seen your sister away from the field, around school with the other girls. She laughs and jokes and has fun just like everyone else. But you guys always treat her like a jock, so how's she suppose to act?" She shifted her books. "You know, until she came along, I never even thought about going out for the boys' team. Now, I'm not sure I really want to. I don't think I can stand to be treated like that." She looked me squarely in the eye. "Do I really have to give up one thing to be another?"

I had no answer. I took a step back and looked her over. For the first time I saw a woman *and* a basketball player. It was quite a combination.

"You know, Janice," I said. "You're right. I had no business even thinking about you the way I did."

Janice blushed. "Oh, Brandon, you don't have to apologize."

"No, I mean it. You had every right to be mad at me, although I'll admit you did pour it on."

"Well," she said sheepishly, "the truth is, I really wasn't all that mad, at least not after the first couple of days. But you seemed so confused, I couldn't help teasing you a little."

"A LITTLE?! Why you!!" I jumped up and slammed my basketball to the sidewalk on the other side of her, simulating my best triple-clutch, double-pump, too-bad-chump, gorilla dunk. "In your face!" I cried, and we both cracked up laughing.

I could've gone on walking with her forever. Unfortunately, forever only comes when you're out shopping with your mother, which means we reached Janice's house much too soon to suit me. We said good-bye, and I floated home on a cloud of serenity. It lasted all through the next day, and I didn't come down until I showed up at Coach Knox's office to help pack for that evening's game. When he saw me, Coach Knox gave a conspiratorial wink, and with a slightly malicious grin he rubbed his hands together. "I'm really looking forward to this," he chuckled. "Yep, I've got a few things up my sleeve this year for 'Old Bull.' "

Old Bull. Coach Knox was referring to "Bull" Slater, the coach of Vanden High School, whom we were playing this week. Vanden High was on the other side of the county, and the rivalry between Coach Knox and Coach Slater was legendary throughout the state. They'd been going after one another for years, and the one constant in their relationship was that Coach Slater always seemed to win. Where Coach Knox's teams were tough, Coach Slater's teams were hardened. Coach Knox's teams were dedicated, Slater's were fanatical. Coach Knox's teams were disciplined, Coach Slater's were militaristic. Coach Knox had never won a state championship, Coach Slater had five to his credit. Coach Slater was a legend, Coach Knox a pretender to the throne.

When the team boarded the bus early Friday afternoon for the trip to Vanden, there was no joking, bantering or smiling. Instead, there was plenty of grumbling and general nastiness. Every player on the team knew what this game meant. This was quite possibly a preview of the state championship game, since we were undefeated and Vanden High had been dive-bombing everything in sight. When we reached our destination, the team hustled into the locker room and got dressed in determined silence. When it was time to take the field, they exploded out of the locker room. I gathered up the equipment and began the long trek out to the field. As I passed through the doorway, Coach Knox stepped up beside me and grabbed the first-aid kit, lightening my load considerably. The funny thing was, he didn't say a word or anything, he just winked and walked on.

As we walked through the gate and into the stadium, a man came over to greet us. It was Coach Slater. You could see immediately why they called him Bull. He was powerfully built, with a thick, muscular neck and a barrel chest. The sheer force of his presence made me want to drop everything and run a couple of laps.

Coach Knox set the first-aid kit down, and the two of them exchanged a firm handshake. "What are you doing there, Knox?" Coach Slater boomed. "That's what you have water boys for, to carry all that stuff."

"Team manager," Coach Knox corrected him. "It's a job that carries with it a great deal of responsibility."

Coach Slater shook his head. "I don't know, Knox, maybe it is true what they've been saying about you, that you've gone soft."

The smile vanished from Coach Knox's face. "What are you talking about?"

It was Coach Slater's turn to smile. "The media's out in full force tonight. There's even camera crews. I guess it's all because of this girl I hear you've got on your team."

"That's right," Coach Knox snapped. "She's my kicker, and a darn good one at that."

Coach Slater looked horrified. "What's come over you, Knox? It's a war out there, man; it's no place for a girl." His eyes narrowed as he looked Coach Knox over long and hard. "You know, it sounds to me like you've lost your guts, Knox."

A chilling silence passed between the two. Finally, Coach Knox spoke. "Don't patronize me, Bull," he said in a slow, measured voice. "I've been in the business too long to take that from you."

Neither man moved. The two of them glared at one another, their nostrils flaring. Finally, Coach Slater turned away. "Just tell that big, bad girl of yours to go easy on my poor, defenseless boys!" he yelled sarcastically as he ran to rejoin his team.

I was a little concerned. I had a feeling that Coach Slater had hit a raw nerve with Coach Knox. Even so, if Coach Knox could only control his emotions and stick to his newly discovered game plan, I knew we'd be okay.

"Lost my guts, have I?" Coach Knox growled as we reached the sideline. "I'll show him what good old-fashioned football's all about." We won the toss and elected to receive. As our offense ran onto the field, Coach Knox grabbed Jim by the arm. "I want you to jam this ball right down their throats this first series."

Uh-oh! Time out! Red lights began flashing off and on in my brain. Sure enough, three plays later we stood minus four yards. So much for "jamming the ball." The entire first quarter was played just like that, with a level of intensity that was breathtaking. It was brutal, physical football, the type that Vanden High excelled at. I didn't like the looks of it. Coach Knox was playing right into their hands.

Then, about midway through the second quarter, our offense got untracked and began a drive. We got down to the forty-yard line before their defense stiffened. Faced with third and four, Coach Knox sent in a dive play. Jim glared over at Coach Knox. The other players grumbled and broke the huddle with about as much enthusiasm as a condemned man shows for his last meal. Not surprisingly, the defense easily stuffed the play for no gain.

I'd seen about as much as I could take. There was no way I could help him if he continually refused to help himself. I sidled over to where he stood. "Hey, Coach, what about opening it up and having fun and all that stuff?"

"But, son, this is fun, this is real football," he protested.

"Coach . . ." I pleaded, as I pointed across the field.

Along the other sideline, Coach Slater was pacing up and down, grabbing players by the face mask, slapping them across their helmet or screaming in their face in an effort to psych them up.

"It's now or never," I said.

Coach Knox watched in stunned silence. "Why, that son of a . . . he's been setting *me* up all these years." He began pacing the sideline like a caged lion. Suddenly, he stopped dead in his tracks. He gritted his teeth and grimaced. "John Lewis!" he hollered. "Get out there for Anderson. Tell them to run the fake-punt pass!"

The punting team lined up. Sarah accepted the

snap from center and aggressively stepped forward. At the last second, as her foot accelerated through the air, she pulled the ball away and tucked it behind her back, exactly the way Coach Knox had showed her in practice the day before. The fake worked beautifully as all eyes shot toward the sky and the Vanden players tried desperately to locate the ball among the stars.

"She's kicked it clear out of sight!" someone yelled from the stands.

Sarah watched with a sly grin on her face. Finally, she pulled the ball out from behind her back and spotted Timmy, who hadn't moved from his position along the line of scrimmage. He was all hunched over with his arms covering his head, undoubtedly praying for the punt not to land anywhere near him.

"Timmy!" she yelled. "I've got the ball right here!"

Timmy's mouth dropped open when he saw Sarah holding the ball. It dropped even further when he realized what she intended to do with it. "Oh, no, you don't!" he cried, backing away. "You're not going to throw that thing at me! Are you?"

"You bet I am. Now start running!"

Timmy looked a little dubious about the whole thing. "Well, if you say so, only don't throw it too hard, okay?"

Timmy took off downfield and Sarah lofted a high, easy floater that he had no problem hauling in. He sprinted down the sideline, with no one on the field any the wiser, and trotted into the end zone untouched.

Having never been on that hallowed ground before, Timmy didn't quite know what to do. He went to spike the ball, but at the last second held back, probably realizing it was much too mundane a gesture. He then held the ball out to one side and began doing the funky chicken. Within seconds, it became obvious that he just didn't have that sort of natural rhythm, so he stopped.

Then, his eyes lit up. He backed up to the goal line and sprinted toward the goal post. I watched in horror as I realized that he intended to spike the ball over the ten-foot-high crossbar. As if that weren't enough, when he jumped, he passed the ball once between his legs and twice behind his back. Not surprisingly, all this motion threw him off-balance and he fell headfirst into the vertical standard, knocking himself unconscious. All I could do was shake my head. Maybe his father was wrong after all. It seemed to me that football wasn't making a man out of Timmy, it was making an idiot out of him.

The thud of cheap plastic on hard metal rang throughout the stadium, catching everyone's attention. The referees ran over and found Timmy still holding the ball as he lay motionless on the ground. It took a minute or two, but when they finally figured out what had happened, they threw their arms into the air, signaling a touchdown.

Our sideline erupted in celebration. The players ran into the end zone and helped Timmy to his feet. Timmy looked a little dazed, but he wore a huge crooked grin on his face and was still clutching the ball tightly as he wobbled off the field.

Even Coach Knox got into the spirit of things. Though he didn't say anything, he smacked Timmy on the back as he passed by. This little love tap sent Timmy sprawling nose first into the turf, but he didn't seem to mind. From the sound of his incoherent babbling he was making fast friends with worms, grasshoppers, ladybugs and assorted other insects down there.

On the other sideline, Coach Slater became so infuriated that he kicked a sideline marker with such force that it sailed through the air and cleared the uprights of the goal posts. The referees threw their arms into the air, signaling the kick good. Our kicking team, already lined up, saw no reason to look a gift horse in the mouth and sprinted off the field, happy to accept the free extra point.

Along the sideline, Coach Knox looked slightly demented. He called the kickoff team together. "Let's onside-kick this one, okay?"

Sarah looked approvingly at Coach Knox. "That's more like it, Flymow. Since when did you grow a brain?"

"Just get out there and do your job, Foots," he growled.

"With pleasure!" she said.

Our kickoff team lined up, and Sarah charged toward the ball. At the last possible second, she let up and gently tapped the ball forward off the tee. It was a perfect fake, with everyone stumbling backward in anticipation of a booming kick. The ball came to rest in an area that had just been vacated. Timmy swooped in from his outside position and dove on it. The referees blew their whistles. Our ball!

That caused Coach Slater to come right out of his shoes. His players dove out of the way as he trashed the entire sideline. He finally roared onto the field.

"What do you think you're doing, Knox!" he bellowed.

Coach Knox grinned. "Why, we're just having a little fun, Slater. What are you guys doing?"

"AAARRGH!!" Coach Slater screamed as he sprinted back toward his sideline, tearing at his hair.

"We've got him now!" Coach Knox cried gleefully. He sprinted over to Jim. His eyes danced with excitement. "Throw the bomb."

Jim took the snap and sprinted out to the right. Just before being plowed under by Vanden's defense, he fired a bullet across the field to Leroy, who had circled out of the backfield and was now sprinting all alone down the left sideline. The ball hit him in full stride and he cruised into the end zone.

Well, as the old saying goes, you can't hit what you can't catch, and that's basically the way the rest of the game went. The poor Vanden High players were so programmed and regimented that they couldn't deal with Coach Knox's sudden inventiveness. He threw everything at them but the kitchen sink, and they spent the rest of the game chasing phantoms as we blew them out 35–7.

When the final gun sounded, we all poured onto the field to exchange handshakes with the Vanden players. Coach Knox looked high and low for Coach Slater, but he was nowhere to be found. Finally, I spotted him at the far end of the track. "There he is, Coach!" I yelled, and we both sprinted over.

When we got there, we found Coach Slater strapped in a straitjacket, being led along passively through a back gate by two men in white suits. When he saw Coach Knox, he straightened up. "I'll get you for this! I'll see you again in the play-offs, and when I do I'll kick your tail!"

Coach Knox walked over and clasped Coach Slater on the shoulder. "You know, Bull, I've got this great idea for a triple reverse pass play. Maybe I'll come down to the hospital and diagram it for you."

Coach Slater went berserk. "I'll kill you, Knox!" he raved, as his eyes rolled up in their sockets. "I'LL KILLAAARRRGH . . . !" One of the attendants stuffed a sock in his mouth to keep him from biting off his tongue.

We stood and watched as they put him into a padded ambulance. Coach Knox shook his head. "Some people just can't take a joke, can they?"

When we got to the locker room, we found it filled with a laughter and joy that had not been present all season. The team quickly showered, dressed and boarded the bus. Sarah made a grand exit from the girls' locker room, accompanied by a mob of young girls who danced around her, busily slamming their bodies into one another and imitating her punting style by slicing their legs through the air in front of them. Sarah looked very relaxed, tousling their hair, exchanging light banter and stopping to sign autographs before getting on the bus.

I couldn't help but smile as we drove away and I watched that rambunctious crowd of girls recede into the distance. I just knew that with Sarah as their patron saint, it was only a matter of time before the Bouncing Bettys of that group began knocking the socks off ball carriers with their hitting rather than with their cheerleading routines. It would be worth the price of admission just to see the look on Coach Knox's face when that day arrived.

The bus ride home was raucous, to say the least. There was lots of laughter and dirty jokes. Timmy stood up in his seat and danced in place, while Leroy expertly coached him on ways to improve his touchdown dance. Coach Knox wandered up and down the aisle, his eyeballs big, stopping every so often to grab a player and ask, "That was fun, wasn't it?" or "Is that really what fun feels like?"

Ferraro seized the opportunity to put his move on Sarah. He marched over, plopped down in the seat next to her and was laying the law down pretty good when she reached forward, seized the front of his shirt and threw him across the aisle, where he landed on top of Leroy.

"Sorry, man," Ferraro apologized, as he separated himself from Leroy. "It feels like I'm trying to climb Mount Everest. Every time I go past base camp, I get clobbered by an avalanche."

Leroy glanced over at Sarah, who was now staring out her window and into the darkness. He let out a low whistle. "That ain't no mountain, that's a volcano. You'd better be careful or she'll do a Mount Saint Helens right on your head!"

"Yeah, thanks for the encouragement," Ferraro said. He then showed us his I'm-a-whipped-dog move, in which he crawled to the back of the bus on all fours and stayed there, licking his wounds for the rest of the journey home.

About the time we pulled into the school parking lot, someone suggested that we all head over to Pietro's, a pizza place, for a little postgame celebration. After hustling into the locker room and stowing our gear, we were off.

All except for Jim. "Hey, I'll meet you guys down there," he said. "I've got to go pick someone up first."

"Some sweet, innocent young thing, no doubt," Leroy said.

"Are there any other kind?" Jim asked, with a twinkle in his eyes, as he disappeared into the darkness.

The rest of us piled into a couple of cars and raced down the road until we reached Pietro's. Once inside, we pulled together some tables and proceeded to chow down.

I was in hog heaven. Everything seemed perfect. I literally sucked down my first piece of pizza and was hard at work on the second when a voice jarred me out of my reverie.

"Hi, Brandon! How are you tonight?"

I looked up. It was Janice! And she was with my brother Jim! I was so startled I dropped the pizza right into my lap. I couldn't believe it. Jim's self-satisfied smirk and Janice's beaming smile confirmed that the night of my greatest triumph had just been transformed into my worst nightmare.

CHAPTER 11

"How could you go out with that slimeball?" I demanded the instant Janice sat down in world history class on Monday morning.

"Brandon!" she scolded. "How can you talk about your brother like that?"

"It's easy. I live with him. I know what kind of lowlife worm he really is."

Janice looked irritated. "Don't be ridiculous. He is not a lowlife worm." Her eyes narrowed. "Besides, you could have asked me out instead."

My mind boggled. She was right, I could have! "Well, uh . . . gee, it never even occurred to me."

"So I've noticed." Her words cut through me like a knife. "But that's beside the point. It did occur to Jim, and he asked me out. That's all there is to it."

"Well, you didn't let him do anything, did you?" I asked accusingly.

Janice's mouth dropped open. "*Brandon!* I . . . I'm shocked. It's none of your business what went on between us."

I couldn't help myself, I went wild. "So you did! You did! Oh, I just knew it! I knew it!"

Janice grabbed my arm and shook me. "Calm down, Brandon. Everyone is staring at us."

I looked around. The amused grins of my classmates lit up the entire room. I took a couple of deep breaths and tried to regain my composure.

"That's better," Janice said. "Now, for your information, nothing happened Friday night. All he did was kiss me good night."

"He . . . he . . . *he kissed you good night?*"

In my rage, I exploded to my feet. Unfortunately, I was still in my desk when I did. I got all tangled up, and while struggling frantically in midair, I lost my balance and fell to the floor, with the desk crashing down on top of me.

As I reached out to throw the stupid contraption off, I felt a sharp pressure against my neck. I looked up. Mr. Clark had me pinned to the floor with one of those long rubber-tipped pointers.

139

He looked very unhappy. "Mr. Lewis!" he said sternly. "I've had to tolerate your increasingly boorish behavior throughout this semester, and, frankly, I'm getting tired of it. Now, you have two choices. You can either agree to conduct yourself in a more civilized fashion in the future or I can end your miserable little existence right here and now by severing your jugular vein. Think carefully about this, Mr. Lewis. It's only fair to warn you that nothing would bring me greater satisfaction than to watch the blood gush from your repulsive little body. It would serve to graphically illustrate to the other miserable wretches in this room that silence is indeed golden. Do I make myself clear?"

I was in no position to argue. I'll have to give him credit, this was one very captivating lecture. I rose up to speak. "Well, I . . ." but a quick jab from the pointer slammed my head back to the floor.

"No, Mr. Lewis, just stay where you are, keep your mouth shut and think about it for the rest of the period." He glanced around the room. The class shot upright in their seats, looking very attentive. "Very good, class," Mr. Clark approved. "Now, as I was saying: In medieval Europe in the thirteenth century, just before the onset of the black plague, we find . . ."

It's hard to act natural when you're lying upside down on the floor, held captive by a madman with a lethal weapon, but I gave it my best shot. When the bell finally rang, Mr. Clark let me up, although not before giving some serious thought to keeping me there for the rest of the day to serve as an example to all the "miserable wretches" in his other classes. When I got outside, Janice was waiting for me.

"Oh, Brandon! That was soooo funny!"

"I'm glad you found it amusing." I stared at her accusingly. "I'll have you know I don't intend to take this lying down."

"But you already have."

"You know what I mean! I'll make Jim sorry he ever set eyes on you. This is war!"

A pleased smile came to Janice's face. "A war? Over me? Oh, Brandon, that sounds like fun!"

Unfortunately, having spoken the words, I had to figure a way to carry them out. I suppose killing Jim would have been the obvious thing to do, but the way the team was playing, I hated to break their momentum.

That Friday, we absolutely hammered Jefferson High. Coach Knox began the game with an onside kick, then followed up with a triple reverse pass, which resulted in a quick score. At that point it was all over but the shouting. I mean, you can't stop something if you have no idea what's coming. Heck, half the time we didn't even know what to expect, with Coach Knox chuckling and chortling his way along the sideline, sending in one bizarre play after another. It really wasn't like him to act this way, and I suppose I should have seen it clearer at the time, starting with the Vanden game, but the truth is, when the scoreboard is racking up points like a pinball machine, it's hard not to get caught up in the excitement.

And rack them up we did. The entire team had played great, but Jim's performance had been exceptional. He'd thrown for close to three hundred yards and four touchdowns. The locker room rocked with excitement after the game, but I have to admit I had very ambivalent feelings. I was really excited about the team's continued success, but I didn't see how I could ever win over Janice's affection if Jim continued to play like that.

That didn't stop me from trying. But the proverbial door had been opened, and Jim walked through it every chance he got. I'd walk Janice home from school one day, Jim would drive her home the next. I'd sit with her at lunch, Jim would take her out to dinner. At the next game I lugged all my equipment out to the field and waved to Janice. Jim blew kisses to her as he threw three touchdown passes and we slaughtered Delta High 45–12.

I was rapidly turning into a nervous wreck. Worse yet, I suddenly couldn't hit my jump shot any longer. The guys from the varsity team were starting to win my lunch money in pickup games. My balance was off, my rhythm destroyed, and no matter how hard I tried, I couldn't seem to get it back.

One day after football practice, while shooting around and consistently clanking the ball off the front rim, someone behind me let out a long, low whistle.

"Boy, I've never seen you shoot that badly before," Sarah commented as she walked over. "Maybe you should concentrate a little more on your follow-through."

"Naw, that wouldn't make any difference. The only thing that'll help me now is to give up the sport. C'mon, let's go home."

As we walked along in silence, Sarah stared at me. "Is there something wrong, Brandon?" she finally asked. "You've been acting kind of funny lately."

"I'm just having a bad day, that's all." A million things ran through my mind as we continued on home. My life had been turned upside down and nothing seemed to make sense anymore. Finally, I turned to Sarah and asked, "Do you know anything about love?"

"Love?!" She sounded disgusted. "Let me tell you one thing about love. From what I've seen, love is nothing but having some guy grabbing at you and slobbering all over your face while he tries to chew your hair off."

"Really?" Boy, I had a lot to learn! I didn't even have the first clue on how to go about chewing a girl's hair off. Were you supposed to start from the scalp or from the end and work your way up? No wonder I couldn't keep up with Jim.

"Oh, yeah," Sarah went on. "Love is nothing but a big wrestling match that's caused by overactive glands. It's pretty disgusting." Suddenly, her eyes lit up. "Brandon, why are you asking me this? Are you in love?"

I thought about it for a moment, but my feelings for Janice didn't sound anything like what Sarah had just described. "No, I guess not," I answered.

"Well, good. Just take my advice. If you ever fall in love, jump into a cold shower and it'll go away. Believe me, you'll be better off without it."

When we arrived home, I ran right upstairs, turned the cold water in the shower on full blast and dove in. Sarah was right, it did go away, only I couldn't really tell what *it* was since my entire body immediately went numb.

For the next couple of days I tried to follow Sarah's advice. I forgot about love and turned my attention to something equally beyond my comprehension: Coach Knox.

My concern about him was beginning to crystallize. With each passing day he was drifting farther and farther from reality. It happened so quickly that

144

it was on top of us before I even realized it. Coach Knox never yelled anymore, he always smiled. He walked around with his shirt hanging half out of his pants. On top of his head, the tiny crew-cut hairs jutted out in a million different directions. He looked an awful lot like an extremely dangerous person who'd been given massive amounts of drugs to keep him under control.

It had me worried. I didn't see how Coach Knox could continue on like that; he was too far out of character. I began to wonder if it wasn't related to his new style of play—if in forcing that on him I hadn't pushed him from one extreme to the other.

On the other hand, because of the change, our team was really hot. The players were having a great time with this newfound style of football, and they were confident that we were going all the way. Every day at practice, I was congratulated for my bright ideas. My brothers even ceased making noises about using me as the next unmanned probe to Jupiter.

We ran our record to 7-0 by slaughtering Edison High, then followed that up with a 38-0 trouncing of St. Mary's, a defeat so devastating that I heard some very un-Christian words escape the lips of the nuns and priests who were in the stands.

Our last game of the regular season was against Meridian Prep. At practice on Monday, the team briskly ran through the exercises. When they were finished, Coach Knox yelled out, "Okay, everyone over here! Boy, did I draw up some goodies this weekend. You're going to love these. First, there's the . . ."

"Say, Coach, aren't you forgetting something?" John interrupted.

Coach Knox looked at his whistle, his clipboard and the football he had in his hand. "Uh, no, son, I think I've got it all right here."

"No, no," John protested. "I'm talking about conditioning. You know, Burma Roads, nut-busters. Don't you think we should do a few?"

Coach Knox screwed up his face. "Aw, those aren't any fun. Let's skip them."

John looked confused. "But, Coach, what about all those things you used to talk about? You know, courage, desire, pride and dedication."

Coach Knox thought about it for a moment. "Well, I suppose you're right. Okay, go ahead."

"But aren't you forgetting something?"

"Why do you keep asking me that?" Coach Knox said in an irritated voice as he frantically looked around. Finally, the light popped on in his head. "Oh, that's right! ON THE GOAL LINE!" he roared.

The players quickly lined up and waited. Coach Knox yelled, "You guys run however much you think you need. I'll be over here when you're done." He threw down his clipboard, turned and fired a pass in my direction. "C'mon, Brandon, let's play catch."

With John serving as Coach Knox, Jr., they ran until their tongues hung out, but stopped short of dropping like flies. When they were done, they all gathered around Coach Knox.

His face was aglow. "Let me tell you, gentlemen," he said while rubbing his hands together and licking his chops, "we are going to end this regular season with a bang."

Poor Meridian Prep, it never had a chance. On the first play of the game, Coach Knox came out with a play where our center and Jim were the only two players over the ball. Everyone else lined up on the other side of the field. The Meridian Prep players just about had a collective heart attack when they saw that. They didn't know where to line up. While their coaching staff signaled wildly for a time-out, the players ran around like chickens with their heads cut off, colliding with one another and getting hopelessly confused.

Jim took the snap from center and threw the ball across the field to Leroy, who had a wall of blockers in front of him. The Meridian Prep defense was so spread out that they were no match for this concentration of manpower, though many of them made it even easier by falling to their knees and weeping in the face of this onslaught. Leroy cruised easily downfield for a touchdown.

The game was a blowout, and the scene was lively in the locker room afterward. The players danced, shouted and generally carried on like maniacs, which, of course, they were. They felt that they were the baddest high school football team ever. Not that I could blame them. I felt the same way. I sat down on a bench, leaned back and admired my handiwork. We were 9-0 and storming into the play-offs.

CHAPTER 12

I was walking out to the field for our first practice in preparation for the play-offs when I heard John cry, "But I don't want to run with the football!"

"Nonsense, son," Coach Knox reassured him. "You'll do just fine."

The panic grew in John's eyes. "But I'm an offensive lineman, not a running back, remember?"

An understanding smile remained on Coach Knox's face. "That's just it, son. You've been in the trenches all season long, doing one heckuva job for this team. It's your turn to have a little fun."

"I'm sorry, Coach, but that wouldn't be any fun.

149

I wouldn't know what to do, lined up in the backfield with Leroy."

Coach Knox shook his head. "Don't be silly, son. No one wants you in the backfield. We're going to have you run the ball from your position on the line."

"WHAT?!" Thirty or so voices rang out. The players exchanged worried glances. John looked like he was about to faint.

"Sure!" Coach Knox bubbled. "We're going to run the fumblerooski play. You know the one." He was met by a mass of blank stares. "You don't? Well, gather around—I'll show you how it works."

As the team packed in around him, Sarah sidled up to me. "Looks like it's finally happened: Old Flymow's gone looney tunes on us."

"I know," I said. "This style of football is too much for him. I don't think he can fit it into any framework he's ever known so it's pushed him to an extreme. Something's got to be done. I don't think he can go on like this."

Sarah dismissed my concerns with the wave of a hand. "You worry too much, Brandon. Take it from me, everything's going to be just fine. Just look around. Everyone out here is having a great time. Even Flymow."

I just shook my head. You see, I knew that this was not Coach Knox's kind of fun; he was operating on borrowed time. I guess the real truth was that I'd kind of grown fond of him. Oh, sure, he'd been a little excessive at times, and maybe he did tend to make Rambo look like a wimp, but at least he was honest enough to listen and take my advice about opening it up. And now, because of me, he was flirting with real danger. It made me want to kick myself in the rear. I'd just wanted to modify his behavior; I never meant to turn him into a raving lunatic.

It bothered me so much that after practice I decided to venture up to Coach Knox's office and have a few words with him. When I got to his door, I heard cries of "Come on, come on, get around that end" and "How can you expect to win football games tackling like that?" I was glad to hear that, in his office, Coach Knox was still in control of himself. I knocked.

"Door's open!" he yelled from within.

I walked in, fully expecting to find the lights off and Coach Knox scrutinizing game films. Instead, he was hunched over his desk, playing with an electronic video football game. "You ever try one of these, son?" he asked, looking up for a second. "Boy, they're great, just great. You can score a million points. Wanna try?"

"Uh, gee, no thanks, Coach," I answered. "Say, shouldn't you be working on a game plan for Friday? You know, looking at films, doing charts and all that?"

Coach Knox set the video game down. "Why bother, son? After all, the name of the game's fun, right? Sitting here in the dark, squinting at those tiny little people on that sixteen-millimeter film, all you wind up doing is hurting your eyes. Besides, we know what we're going to do this Friday: reverses, alley-oops, flea flickers. " A gleam came to his eyes. "Even the old fumblerooski!" He fell back into his seat, slapped his knee and started to cackle.

I backed toward the door. I'd seen enough to know he was beyond help. "Uh, yeah, great fun, Coach. Well, I'll see you later. I've got to be going."

"Okay, Brandon, see you later." He picked up his football game and began furiously pushing buttons. "That's it . . . that's it . . . suck 'em in . . . throw it . . . NOW! Yeah, touchdown!" He jumped to his feet, threw his arms into the air and began dancing in place. "Oh, this is great, just great. We're scoring at will tonight."

As I closed the door to his office and walked down the stairs, I felt a little like Dr. Frankenstein. That Friday evening, the monster reared its ugly head. We were playing Franklin High, a pretty good team from across the valley. Unfortunately for them, they'd never faced a team coached by a maniac before.

We easily stuffed Franklin High on its first possession, and after we received the punt, its defense played with an intensity born from desperation. Their players realized that they simply couldn't afford to fall behind early. On first and second downs, they stopped us with a hustling, swarming defense. It was third and ten when Coach Knox grabbed one of our tight ends, whispered "fumblerooski" in his ear and pushed him onto the field.

The offense broke the huddle, and as they headed to the line of scrimmage, John turned and grabbed hold of Jim. "C'mon, Jim," he pleaded, "don't make me do it. Run it up the middle, throw the bomb, anything." He dropped to his knees and latched onto Jim's leg.

Jim tried to pull away. "Knock it off, John, this is embarrassing. Everyone in the place is staring at us."

"I don't care. I don't want to do it."

Jim reached down, grabbed John by the front of his jersey and yanked him to his feet. "Quit your whining!" he yelled. "Everyone else on this team's had to make sacrifices this year. What are you, special? Now, get in there and score your touchdown like a man."

John shuffled up to the line of scrimmage and got down into a three-point stance. "I really don't want to score a touchdown," he told the defensive lineman who was lined up opposite him.

"Huh?"

John didn't get a chance to explain further, because just then the ball was snapped. The ball came up to

Jim's hands, but instead of closing on it, he kept his palms open so that it hit against them and fell straight to the ground. He then spun to the right and faked as though he were pitching the ball back to Leroy. At the same time, everyone along the line pulled out and took off in that direction, setting up the classic "student body" right-end sweep. The Franklin High defense reacted immediately, furiously fighting through blockers to get at Leroy.

John, on the other hand, held his ground for just a moment, then pulled out to the left, against the grain. He scooped the ball up from the ground and turned upfield, all alone. There was mass confusion on the part of the Franklin High players as they descended on Leroy and realized that he didn't have the ball. It took a few seconds for them to figure out what had happened, but by then it was too late; John was already a good twenty yards downfield, nervously glancing over his shoulder as he thundered along. Upon reaching the end zone, he ran over to the referee and thrust the ball at him as though it were a stick of dynamite. He then charged over to the sideline and launched himself under the bench, where he curled up and cowered.

Coach Knox went crazy. "The old fumblerooski! What a play, what a play!" He grabbed my arms and began dancing, pulling me along with him. "Oh, this is great fun, isn't it, son?" He let go of me, ran over to the bench and crawled underneath it. "You see, son," he said, squeezing up next to John. "It wasn't so bad, was it? It was fun, son, fun!"

Well, as you can imagine, that was the straw that broke Franklin High's back. It had absolutely no idea how to deal with craziness of that degree, so the players merely shrugged their shoulders, accepted their beating with dignity and went home to start working on next year.

In the locker room after the game the players were relatively tame. They all realized that this was just the first step. Coach Knox, on the other hand, was ecstatic. His eyes were as big and bright as full moons as he hopped around the benches, clasping players on the shoulders. "Great game, great game!" he announced. "That was fun, wasn't it? Boy, do I have some great ideas for next week's game. Next week's game? My goodness, I'd better get to work on that!"

Every pair of eyes in the room followed him as he bounded down the aisle and up the stairs and disappeared into his office.

"Boy," Jim said, shaking his head, "I'm beginning to think I liked him better the other way."

John was trembling slightly. "Yeah, I can hardly wait to see what he dreams up next."

It didn't take long, because as I was walking out to the field the next Monday for our first practice in preparation for the semifinal play-off game, I heard

John cry, "But I don't want to catch the football!"

"Nonsense, son," Coach Knox reassured him. "You'll do just fine."

The panic grew in John's eyes. "I don't want to do just fine, Coach. I'm an offensive lineman, not a . . ."

I couldn't help but feel I'd heard this conversation before. Sure enough, within minutes, the tape and pads were gone from John's hands and Coach Knox was trying to show him how to catch a football.

Once Coach Knox had satisfied himself that he'd done all he could with John, he went on to other things, and the remainder of practice moved along pretty rapidly, as was usually the case these days. When the whistle finally blew an end, I gathered up the equipment and headed in with everyone else.

As I meandered along, Ferraro trotted by and joined Sarah, who was just up ahead. They walked together for a while, seemingly engaged in pleasant conversation, when suddenly Sarah's face darkened. She said something to Ferraro that caused his soft smile to deteriorate into a look of desperate confusion. Being the sort who just loves a good argument, I hurried to get within earshot.

"Aw, c'mon, Sarah," Ferraro was saying, "give me one good reason why you won't."

"Because I don't want to," she replied pugnaciously. "And that's the best reason I can think of."

Ferraro roughly latched onto Sarah's arm and spun her toward him. "I'm getting tired of your games," he said angrily. "I've tried everything I can think of, but you won't even give me a chance. I don't get it. What have I got to do to satisfy you?"

Sarah stuck a finger into Ferraro's chest. "Just get out of my life—that would be a great start."

Sarah stormed off. Ferraro just stood and stared. "Boy, she sure does a good job of playing hard to get."

A little while later, I was out behind the gym, shooting my basketball once again in hopes of regaining the form that I'd so totally lost. Sarah stepped out of the girls' locker room, watched my pathetic performance for a moment, then walked over. "Here, Brandon, give me that thing," she ordered.

I fed her a bounce pass, and she pulled up from twenty feet. There was a loud clank as the ball hit the rim and bounced away. Sarah stared for a moment in disbelief, then ran over and retrieved the ball. She came dribbling back, did a quick spin and threw up a fifteen-foot fadeaway jumper. Again, she caught the iron flush, and this time the ball ricocheted straight to me. She glared at the rim as though it were somehow at fault. "Well, that just proves what I've always said," she growled. "Basketball's a dumb sport. C'mon, let's go."

Sarah seemed uncommonly subdued as we walked

along. "What was that all about with you and Ferraro after practice?" I asked.

"Oh, nothing," she answered. "The school's planning a dance for after the state championship game, if we get that far. Ferraro asked me if I'd go with him."

"And you said no?"

"Of course I said no." She sounded insulted. "Why would I go out with him?"

"Well, he seems like a nice enough guy."

"Are you kidding? He's only interested in one thing." She waved a finger in my direction. "Let me tell you something. You've got to cut a guy like that off at the knees, otherwise he'll never let up. If I didn't slap him down regularly, he'd be on me like ugly on a frog."

As we walked along in silence, I stared at the side of Sarah's face. I was getting some real weird vibes. A tingling sensation gnawed at the base of my neck. I thought about what she'd just said, and I thought about the past few weeks and months; my walks and talks with Janice, my competition with Jim, the conversations with Sarah, my jump shot, Coach Knox . . .

Then it hit me. Of course! I looked at Sarah. I didn't see a woman. I didn't see a jock. For the first time I saw a . . . "Hey, Sarah, wait a minute! I . . . I don't think that's what Ferraro's after. If that's all he was interested in, don't you think he'd have quit trying long ago?"

Sarah scoffed. "Oh, don't be so dumb, Brandon. That's all any guy is interested in."

"No, I really don't think so." I slapped myself in the forehead. "Oh, why did I ever listen to you? You've got it all backward. No wonder I blew it with Janice."

"Janice . . . Janice." Suddenly, Sarah's eyes grew big. "Janice Johnson? The cheerleader? You've got the hots for that girl Jim's been going out with? Well, no wonder you've been walking around like you just lost your best friend."

"But I haven't lost my best friend!" I protested. "And she's not just a cheerleader, that's the point. Boy, you really screwed me up the last time we talked, and it's taken until this very moment for me to figure it out."

Sarah stopped dead in her tracks and gave me a puzzled look.

"Let me ask you a question," I continued. "Do you want to be judged your whole life on how well you kick a football or a soccer ball or whatever?"

Sarah sneered. "What a stupid question. Of course not."

"Well, then, why don't you start acting like it?"

"What . . ."

"Yeah, it's like this thing with Ferraro. You know,

I think all he really wants to do is go out and have a good time, nothing more. He's the first one who's ever seen you as anything but a jock. He saw it even before I did." I shook my head. "And all this time I thought he was just a big, dumb linebacker."

Sarah stared at me like I'd just called a triple reverse, fake field goal, pass-punt.

"Look, this isn't a game," I continued. "You've proven everything there is to prove. You said you wanted to be like everyone else; here's your chance. Just lighten up and go out with Ferraro. Just once. Do it for yourself. Do it . . . do it, just for kicks."

Sarah looked dubious. "Just for kicks?

"Yeah, just for kicks."

"Boy, I don't know . . ." She shook her head as she wandered away. I was a little concerned, because at that moment, with her body language and the look on her face, she looked an awful lot like Coach Knox.

I picked up my ball. I turned and noticed a couple of young kids playing on one of the hoops. I stopped and watched. They were pretending to be Larry Bird and Magic Johnson. Peals of laughter echoed off the school buildings as they imitated moves and threw up all sorts of weird shots. A smile stretched across my lips and soon engulfed my entire face. I quickly ran over and joined them. I pulled up for an eighteen-foot jump shot and buried one. I quickly retrieved the ball and let loose from three-point range. Again, the sweet sound of a swish. I hit fifteen straight jumpers, and when I capped it all off with a driving, three-sixty, double-clutch bank shot over Kareem Abdul-Jabbar, I knew I'd made it all the way back.

The next day, during lunch, I marched into the cafeteria and sat down across from Janice. She looked up from her plate of . . . well, I'm not sure what it was—you know how it is with cafeteria food.

Her face lit up when she saw me. "Brandon! What a pleasant surprise! Where have you been hiding?"

I thought about it for a moment. "You know, I think all this time, I've been hiding from myself. I guess when you do that, no one else can find you either."

Janice looked impressed. "That's a very profound thought, Brandon. Did you just think it up by yourself or did you steal it from a comic book?" Her mock seriousness disintegrated, and she began giggling.

"Hey, don't knock it," I replied indignantly. "I'll have you know, some of my best lines come from comic books."

She rolled her eyes. "I know. Believe me, I know!"

"Why, you . . ." I reached across the table, grabbed her fork and destroyed her Jell-O, mashing it into nothing more than lumpy, green water. The two of us broke up into laughter.

The rest of the day was pure enjoyment. Janice and I did all those things we'd done before: met between classes, exchanged gossip, copied from one another in Spanish class, laughed about Ms. Long's new frizzed hairstyle. Only this time, things were different. I felt very relaxed, very calm. My heart stayed in my chest, my eyes stayed in their sockets and my brain remained unfogged. More important, for the first time, I just went with the flow and had a good time.

At the end of the day, I beat Jim to the punch and walked Janice home. It rained all the way there, and we shared an umbrella. Now, *that* was romantic.

The rest of the week went pretty much the same way. We spent hours and hours together. I'd never had so much fun in my entire life. But before I even had the chance to catch my breath, Friday rolled around and I was forced to turn my attention and energies to something that had become even more wild and unpredictable than mere love. That thing was football.

CHAPTER 13

A sense of quiet confidence pervaded the atmosphere as we prepared to play Ulysses S. Grant High School in the state semifinal play-off game. And with good reason, because right from the very beginning, Coach Knox hit them with everything but the kitchen sink. There were flanker reverses, alley-oop passes, the old U-Cal rugby play. John even caught a pass and scored on a tackle eligible, though he almost had a heart attack when the play was called and we had to burn a time-out while everyone in the huddle convinced him he had no choice but to do it. Grant was never in the game, and we absolutely hammered them

38-0. It was an incredible feeling. We were headed for the state championship game! After some heavy celebrating in the locker room, we all decided to meet down at Pietro's.

Sarah, Jim, John and I were already up to our mouths in pizza when the rest of the team began filing in. Ferraro came through the door, wandered around for a moment, then meekly sidled over to where we were sitting. "Uh, hi, Sarah. Mind if I sit here?" he asked, gesturing to the empty seat across from her.

Sarah shot a look in our direction, but we all were busy whistling and looking up at the ceiling. "Um, sure, I suppose so," she said.

Ferraro eagerly sat down. "Quite a football game tonight, huh?" he commented.

"I've seen better . . ." Sarah caught herself. She chuckled. "No, that's not true. I don't think I've ever seen a team play better than we did tonight."

Ferraro cleared his throat. "Hey, Sarah, I've been thinking about it, and, well, there's something I'd like to say to you." He took a deep breath. "It's been a long season, Sarah, and let's face it, we've been through a lot together. But there's something I want to tell you, something I've wanted to say all along. Sarah, I love . . ."

"You what!?" Sarah sprang to her feet.

"I love your cut block!"

Sarah froze in place. "My cut block?" she cried.

"Yeah. I really get off on the way you flatten people with it. You think maybe someday before practice you could show me your technique on that?"

Sarah was totally confused. "Uh, well, sure, Ron, I could do that." She looked over at me and, seeing as how it had worked every other time this season, I gave her the old thumbs-up sign. "You know, Ron," she continued, "I really admire that forearm shiver of yours. The way it rattles the teeth of the opposition sends a tingle up my spine."

Ferraro looked pleased. "It does?"

"Yeah, I've been meaning all season to have you show me the right way to do it."

Ferraro's grin stretched from ear to ear. "Oh, it's easy. First, you start by bringing your arm back to here . . . stand up and let me show you."

He grabbed Sarah's arm and helped her to her feet. Within minutes the two of them were knocking over chairs, tables and waitresses as they busily exchanged tips, techniques and old war stories.

About five pizzas and an hour later, Pietro's had pretty much cleared out. Sarah and Ferraro were talking quietly across the table. Finally, Sarah turned to me. "Say, Brandon. Ron and I are going to the dance after the championship game next week. Why don't you and Janice come with us, you know, double date."

Wow, what a great idea! "Hey, I'd love to! I'll just . . ."

Jim's laughter cut me off. "Quit dreaming, kid.

165

She's not going anywhere with you. She's going to that dance with me."

My heart stopped beating. "You asked her to the dance?"

Jim snickered evilly. "Not yet I haven't, but I'm going to right now. Thanks for the idea, chump!" He leaped out of his chair and sprinted from the restaurant.

The bottom fell out of my stomach. I felt sick. Can you believe it? Losing the girl three times, that must have been some kind of age-group world record. I felt like dying.

I walked home in a daze, and when I got there I decided to commit suicide by watching *Three's Company* reruns. I was about twenty minutes into the program and fading fast, when Jim burst through the front door.

"She said no!" he roared. "Can you believe it? She had the nerve to say no to me, the star quarterback. Why, that ungrateful . . ." He disappeared around the corner and into the kitchen. When he reappeared, he was chomping away on a roast beef sandwich. "Well, looks like I'll just have to call up Bouncing Betty."

It took a moment for it to sink in, but once it did, I shot straight up out of the chair. I was out the front door before my feet even hit the ground, and I didn't slow down until I reached Janice's house. When I got there, I bounded up on the front porch and pounded on the door.

When Janice finally answered, her mouth fell open. "Why, Brandon, what are you doing here at this time of night? It's quarter past . . ."

"You said no to Jim?" I gasped, while trying to catch my breath.

"You mean about the dance? Well, of course I said no."

I felt like I'd missed something. "But what about all those times you went out with him? I thought you really liked him."

"I do like him, Brandon," she said. "He's very nice. What girl wouldn't want to go out with a star football player who also happens to be the most gorgeous guy around? Everyone has fantasies, and it was fun while it lasted, but you know something? I found out that fantasies aren't real."

"So you'll do it?"

"Do what?" she asked.

"Go to the dance with me!" I almost screamed.

Her eyes sparkled. "Why, Brandon, I thought you'd never ask. Of course I'll go to the dance with you." She leaned out of the doorway and kissed me.

It's kind of hard to describe a moment like that, and since I'm not an exhibitionist I don't think I will. Let's just say I kind of liked the way things were turning out. After all, I'd just gotten the girl and at the same time finally managed to put Jim in his place. I'd even succeeded in bringing Sarah and Ferraro together. All that remained was for Coach Knox to straighten out and we'd have a happy ending for sure.

Unfortunately, a happy ending was going to be a lot tougher than it looked. I say that because the next morning when I picked up the newspaper, I read that Vanden High had destroyed Hillcrest High 38-6 in the other semifinal play-off game.

When I saw that, my heart sank. It seemed too large a coincidence. Bull Slater would be getting his rematch after all. And this time it would be for all the marbles.

I was scared to death. In his present condition Coach Knox was no match for a runaway train like Bull Slater. It was obvious that he'd totally lost it and was in danger of never finding it again. He'd reached the point where he was still passing Go, but was no longer collecting the two hundred dollars. And this time Old Bull would be ready. He would've dissected the game films by now and found a way to take all that craziness and unpredictability, turn it around and use it to bury Coach Knox.

Something just had to be done. I was more than just a little responsible for Coach Knox's current condition. The ball was back in my court again. There just had to be a way to solve this problem once and for all. It set me to thinking. . . .

That evening after dinner, while John, Jim and Sarah were still at the table, I made my move. "What do you think about Coach Knox these days?" I asked. "Pretty looney, huh?"

"Mad as a hatter," Jim chimed in. "So what else is new? He's been crazy since the day he was born."

"I know, but just look at him," I said. "He may have been crazy before, but at least that was really him. Right now, he's in an unnatural state, and if something's not done soon, he's going to crack completely."

"Who cares?" Jim said, dismissing my concerns with the wave of a hand. "In a few days, the season'll be over. We'll have our state championship, and they can haul him off to the funny farm where he should have been all along."

"But it's not fair!" I protested. "Doesn't anything ever penetrate that thick skull of yours? Can't you see the way he's given himself up for the good of the team? We need to help him before it's too late."

Jim got a little irritated. "Hey, who asked you anyway? Why don't you butt out?"

"That's enough, Jim," Sarah cut in. "It's like Brandon said, we've got a problem. Now, how are we going to solve it?"

Jim was incredulous. "You're sticking up for Flymow, after all he's done to you this year?"

"Yeah, old Flymow's been tough this year," she

said. "He's been unreasonable on occasion. But he was just trying to be the best. Besides, we lived through it and now we're going to play for the state championship, so he couldn't have been all wrong."

John jumped in. "She's right, something needs to be done. You may be having fun, Jim, but I'm having a lousy time out there. This isn't real football any more than what we were doing at the beginning of the season. If he tries to make me score another touchdown, I'll have a nervous breakdown."

"Besides, Jim," I added, "you don't really think that Bull Slater's going to let us get away with running trick plays up and down the field again, do you?"

"Oh, yeah, so how's he going to stop us?"

"Well, it seems to me that a good place to start would be to have his defense break both your legs."

That got Jim's undivided attention. "Okay, okay, maybe you are onto something. So, tell me, runt, what's the game plan?"

I rubbed my hands together. "All right, gather around. This is what I have in mind. . . ."

When Friday evening rolled around, we took that long, tense ride to the stadium. When we arrived, our players filed silently into the locker room. Their jaws were set firm, their expressionless faces were cast in stone and their eyes seared like red-hot coals. I felt like I was going to a funeral.

The nervous whimpering and moaning started up almost immediately. Helmets went on early, and a number of players began slamming their heads into the lockers. Growls, grunts and snarls filled the room as game time grew nearer. Finally, there was a knock on the door. One of the referees stuck his head in. "Five minutes!" he said, then quickly ducked out again as a football, a pair of cleats, two oranges and a section of the bench went whizzing past his nose. I could tell the team was ready to play.

Coach Knox got up and walked over in front of the team. "Well, guys, this is it." His eyes drifted around the room. "You know something? For twenty years, I would have killed for this moment, the chance to win a state championship. Twenty long years." He shook his head. "Boy, that's dumb, isn't it? Is anything really worth waiting that long for?" He thought about it for a moment. "Well, that's not important now. We have a game to play. So, just go out there and have a good time."

The team roared out of the locker room in a frenzy. Coach Knox and I walked out together. As we stepped out of the tunnel and onto the artificial turf, we crossed paths with Coach Slater. He was accompanied by a little man in a white lab coat who clutched a huge syringe in one hand.

"Good to see you, Bull," Coach Knox said as he clasped Coach Slater on the shoulder.

Coach Slater spun away. "Get away from me," he snarled, shaking his fist. "Tonight I'm going to take that mumbo-jumbo football of yours and jam it right down your throat. Do you understand?"

From the look on his face, Coach Knox clearly did not. "Uh, gee, Bull, there's no reason to be so hostile. Why don't we go out tonight and try to have some fun, okay?"

Coach Slater became livid. "Fun? Knox, this is for the state championship! Why, I ought to . . ."

As Coach Slater ranted and raved, the little man in the lab coat scurried forward and buried the syringe deep into his hip. Coach Slater let out a yelp and jumped about a foot into the air, but within seconds his eyes glazed over and he began breathing easier.

"I don't know what I'm getting all worked up about, Knox," he said, now very calm. "I've whipped you every other time you've gotten this far and I'll whip you this time, too."

Coach Knox just smiled and nodded. "Gee, Bull, that's great. Good luck to you, too." He stuck his hand out to shake.

Coach Slater growled as he slapped Coach Knox's hand away. The little man in the white lab coat stepped forward. "And keep that thing away from me!" he bellowed, pointing to the syringe.

"Sorry," the little man piped. "Doctor's orders."

"The heck you say!" Coach Slater boomed as he

took off toward the sideline with the little man in hot pursuit.

Amid a deafening roar from the crowd, we received the opening kickoff. Coach Knox started things off by having Jim throw deep. Vanden High had done their homework, double-covering our ends and forcing Jim to throw the ball away. Second and third downs were equally unsuccessful as our double reverse and halfback option were stopped cold. "Fake punt run!" Coach Knox called out to Sarah as our punting unit took the field.

Sarah looked over in my direction. I shook my head no.

The snap was made and with Vanden High covering the flats, looking for something tricky, Sarah stepped forward and unleashed a mammoth kick that drove their punt returner back to his own fifteen-yard line.

As he turned upfield he was greeted by the sight of Timmy, who was bearing down fast. The punt returner obviously knew all about Timmy, because he faked left, faked right, then shuffled his feet, making his ankles a hard target to hit while he tried to gauge where Timmy would land.

Instead of going for the ankles, Timmy lowered his head and blasted the sucker in the chest with a massive hit that rang throughout the stadium. It was all the poor guy could do just to hang on to the ball as he crashed heavily to the turf.

"Way to hit!" "How to stick, Timmy, how to stick!" our players cried as Timmy made it to the sideline. Coach Knox trotted over to where he stood. "What are you doing, son, sticking your head in there like that?" he asked. "Don't you know you could get hurt?"

Timmy looked over at me. I gave him the high sign. "Uh, well, I guess I just got carried away, Coach. Don't worry, it won't happen again."

"Good, good," Coach Knox said, then he sprinted over to where Sarah stood. "What was that all about, Foots? I thought I told you to fake the punt."

"Uh . . . yeah, you did, Flymow. But didn't you see the way they had it covered? I had to kick it away; I didn't have any other choice."

"Well, okay," Coach Knox said. "But do what I say next time. I really wanted to see one of those great alley-oop passes."

Our defense was now on the field, and on the first two plays Coach Knox called for all-out blitzes. With some hand signals, I overruled him and had everyone stay in his position and play it straight up. Vanden High, anticipating some heavy overpursuit, ran a couple of quick trap plays, but we held our ground and stopped them at the line of scrimmage for no gain.

"What's going on out there?" Coach Knox said,

scratching his head. "I signaled for a blitz, didn't I?"

Then, on third down, it happened. Crozier, reading the misdirection play, slid in behind the trap block and blindsided the ball carrier, causing him to cough up the football. We recovered the fumble on their eighteen-yard line.

"Our ball, our ball, Coach!" I yelled. "C'mon, let's ram it down their throats!"

"Don't be ridiculous, Brandon," he scolded. "This is a perfect time for our flea flicker." When Jim got to the huddle, he fired a glance at me. I signaled for an off-tackle run.

On the snap of the ball, John fired off the line and crushed the defensive end like you would an aluminum can. Leroy exploded through the hole, ran right over the strong safety and carried two other defensive players on his back into the end zone. The refs threw their arms into the air. We were on the board!

"What in the heck was that?" Coach Knox looked puzzled. "That sure didn't look like a flea flicker to me."

On the next defensive series, it was more of the same. Coach Knox called for blitzes, and I had the team hold their ground. With Ferraro leading the way, we not only stopped them, we pushed them back. Then, when we got the ball back, it was Leroy left, Leroy right, Leroy up the middle as we systematically moved down the field.

Coach Knox was totally confused. Every play he called turned into something entirely different. "What's going on out there?" he finally cried in exasperation.

I smiled. "Don't you recognize it, Coach?" I said. "It's good old-fashioned football."

His face was a blank. "Good old-fashioned football," he repeated stiffly, then turned back to the action on the field.

John single-handedly caved in the left side of their line.

"Good old-fashioned football."

Third and one. Jim ran a quarterback sneak.

"Good old-fashioned football."

Leroy ran right over two tacklers.

"Good old-fash . . . my goodness!" he exclaimed. "It *is* good old-fashioned football!"

Unconsciously, he reached down and tucked his shirt in. The hairs on his head all of a sudden stood at attention. Just then, Jim pitched out, and five perfectly timed, crushing blocks allowed Leroy to snake down the sideline for another score.

I could swear I saw a tear in the corner of Coach Knox's eye. "Good old-fashioned football," he whispered.

On the other sideline, Coach Slater was not doing nearly so well. He screamed at the top of his lungs and sprinted over to the little man in the white lab coat. He snatched the syringe away from him, then drove it into his own leg, draining every ounce of whatever wonderful medication it contained. He pulled the syringe out, handed it back, then pirouetted and fell flat on his face, out cold.

Coach Knox watched all this in amazement. The next time we gained possession of the ball, he called Jim over to him. "Throw the bomb," he ordered.

"But Coach!" I cried in alarm.

Coach Knox looked at me and smiled. "Don't worry, son, I'm okay now. We're going to throw the bomb only because it's the proper play to call at this point. Agreed?"

I laughed. "You got it, Coach."

Needless to say, the pass went for a touchdown. It was one of the many plays that they'll always talk about, on that day when we beat the invincible Vanden High School Vikings 45-0 while playing "good old-fashioned football."

There's no way I can adequately explain what it feels like to be part of a championship team. I would only hope that everyone could experience such a moment. There's an exhilaration beyond description and yet, at the same time, a knowledge that you'll never quite experience anything like it again. You find yourself desperately wanting to squeeze every last, sweet ounce of enjoyment from the moment. That's how it was in our locker room after the game as we busily danced in each other's arms, exchanged high fives and doused one another with cans of pop.

Coach Knox finally called the team together. He cleared his throat. "I just want to say to all of you that you are the finest group of young men"—he glanced over at Sarah—"and young women that I have ever had the privilege of being associated with. You've shown more pride and more dedication than you'll ever know." He looked over at me. "And, more important, you've taught me how to relax and have a little fun. For that I thank each and every one of you."

"Right on, Coach!" Leroy yelled out. "Tell it like it is!"

That broke Coach Knox up. He laughed, we laughed and, honest to goodness, it made me want to cry.

The bus ride home was just a blur. When we arrived at the school, there was an enormous crowd waiting. They'd already scheduled a big parade for us through town on Monday, but from the way those people carried on, you just knew that the celebration was starting that evening.

We went inside the locker room and ditched our things. When we came out again, the crowd was gone, well on its way to getting the party started. Janice was waiting for me, and she looked absolutely stunning. In her full-length red dress and two gold sweatbands she was the most beautiful woman I'd ever seen.

As we all stood around, waiting for Sarah to re-appear from the girls' locker room, Jim came up and joined us. On his arm was a cute young sophomore girl he'd managed to dig up after Bouncing Betty had also given him the brush-off. It was quite a blow to Jim's ego to have two women turn him down, but he seemed happy enough at that moment.

Just then, who should appear around the corner but Bouncing Betty! "Hi, guys," she said. "Has any-one seen Timmy?"

"Timmy?!"

"Someone call my name?" Timmy asked, as he strolled out of the locker room. His eyes immediately fell on Bouncing Betty. "Ah, Betty! You look lovely! Shall we go?" He stuck his arm out, and she latched on. "Ta-ta," he said as they disappeared around the corner.

Jim's mouth fell open. "W...W...Wait a minute! She turned me down to go to the dance with him? *With him?*" He grabbed his date by the hand and yanked her along. "Hey, Timmy, Timmy! Hold on! I want to talk to you!"

We were still laughing when Sarah came out of the girls' locker room. "Are we ready?" I asked. I put my hand out, and Janice accepted it. Sarah put her arm around Ferraro, and everyone nodded.

As we started off, Coach Knox walked out of the locker room. We nodded as he walked by. He nodded in return. Once he had passed by, we continued on. Then his voice rang out. "Hey, Sarah!"

Sarah looked stunned. It was the first time Coach Knox had ever called her by her real name. She turned around. "Yes, Coach Knox?" she said, returning the favor.

"You know," he said, with a twinkle in his eye, "you'd make one heck of a Marine!"

His soft chuckle stayed with us long after he'd disappeared into the darkness.

EPILOGUE

So, there you have it. Pretty weird, huh? Well, let me tell you, I lived through it and I'm still not sure it really happened.

One thing I am sure of, though, is that life goes on. That's why, the day after the championship game, I was down at the school bright and early, shooting hoops. Practice was scheduled to start Monday, and it never hurts to take a few extra shots.

I was on a run of ten in a row when a pleasant voice sang out, "Hi, Brandon!"

I spun around. Janice! "What are you doing here?" I asked.

She smiled mischievously. "Oh, I thought I'd come down and shoot a few with you."

"Hey, that's great!" I said. "Here."

I tossed her a bounce pass. She pulled up for a twenty-two-foot jump shot and drained it. She ran over, retrieved the ball and fired one up from a bad angle, eighteen feet out, behind the backboard. Again, nothing but net.

With astonishing grace, she scooped up the loose ball and dribbled out beyond the top of the key. She then charged toward the hoop, took off just inside the free-throw line and skyed, higher and higher and higher, until I was afraid she might disappear into the clouds. She zeroed in on the basket, double-clutched and threw down just about the most outrageous gorilla dunk you've ever seen. The ball bounded away crazily as she came back to earth. She turned and smiled at me. I smiled back. I could hardly wait for basketball season to begin.